RISE OF NIGHT

THE CRESCENT CHRONICLES #1

ASHLEY CLAIRE

Introduction

Hi Family, Friends, and Readers!

Ashley here with another extra special content warning for you.

There is minimal smut/spice/sexual content in this one, (it's probably only one pepper on the scale— but give me a break this is a trilogy and a slooooowwwww burn). I don't think this one will change the way you look at me over the potatoes at Thanksgiving, but if you're still worried about it, feel free to put the book down now.

Thanks, Love you bunches!

XOXO, Gossip Girl — whoops, I mean, Ashley.

Real Content Warnings:

- Suicidal Thoughts
    - Depression
    - Anxiety
    - Violence
    -Death/Murder
    -Grief
    -Explicit Content & Language

-Sexual Activity
-Unwanted Advances

I do need to point out that while this book isn't spicy, it does have a lot of suicidal thoughts and depression.

Which is normal for someone in Elliora's situation, however, if you or someone you know is experiencing depression or suicidal thoughts, please reach out to the suicide hotline, and dial 988.

You matter, your feelings matter, and it's okay to share your feelings.

Please take care of yourself and your mental health, because I care about every person who picks up this book. This world needs you in it.

To anyone who ever looked up at the night sky and thought "I wish dragons were real", this one's for you. Dragons may not be real, but magic is, because love exists.

Rise of Night Playlist

- **Rewrite the Stars**
  The Piano Guys

- **Who's Afraid of Little Old Me?**
  Taylor Swift

- **Nights Like This**
  The Kid LAROI

- **Ode to the Blue Sky**
  Praam

- **Kill them All**
  Ramin Djawadi

- **The Silence**
  Morgan Clae

- **Someone you loved**
  Lewis Capaldi

- **I See Fire**
  Ed Sheeran

- **Neverland**
  Zendaya

- **Game of Survival**
  Ruelle

- **Night Changes**
  One Direction

- **All the Stars**
  Kendrick Lamar, SZA

- **In the Stars**
  Benson Boone

- **Skyborne**
  Annie Rosier & Daniel Paterok

- **War of Hearts**
  Ruelle

- **I love you I'm sorry**
  Gracie Abrams

- **I found**
  Amber Run

- **You should see me in a crown**
  Billie Ellish

- **Let me Go**
  Benson Boone

- **loml**
  Taylor Swift

DAY REALM
SWAYLIN
SOLARA
SEA OF WANDERERS
DUSK DISTRICT

SHADOW KINGDOM
THE UMBRA CITADEL
THE GREAT DIVIDE
NIGHT REALM
CANOPUS
VN DOMAIN
GULF OF THE DEEP
N
NW
NE
W
E
SW
SE
S

Prologue

ELLIORA STARES AT THE sparkling blue sea as she sails across the Sea of Wanderers. Her strawberry blonde hair whips around in the cool breeze. She is aboard a ship of about one hundred males and females of different races from all across Swaylin, all destined for the Night Realm.

Elliora is on her way, just as every other summoned Swaylini before her. Her own mother, Naiobi, had ventured to the Night Realm shortly after her nineteenth birthday and returned home pregnant with Elliora a year later. Her grandfather always said that was when her mother lost all the sanity she had left.

Various members of Swaylin receive summons to the Night Realm shortly after their nineteenth birthday, and from what Elliora can see, there doesn't seem to be any rhyme or reason to who gets summoned. She and her mother are just two of the unfortunate souls to receive the summons.

Most who are summoned don't return from the Night Realm, and those who do are never the same. Elliora has spent her whole life wondering if those who don't return have passed on to a new life, or if they still reside somewhere within the Night Realm.

No one in Swaylin speaks of Night. It is daylight twenty-four hours a day in Swaylin, and it's believed that even speaking of Night will automatically cause you to be summoned. No person of Swaylin wants to be summoned, and therefore Night is not heard of.

Elliora doesn't know how this all began. They don't teach the history or explain why everyone must obey the summoning without question.

Elliora has heard whispers, though, of the Night Realm and what its skies might look like. The tales talk of stars, of the glimmering silver and white specks that are rumored to be dead souls, and are now trapped against a backdrop of pure black. Elliora had seen them in her dreams and made the mistake of telling her mother. Her mother told her then, when she was twelve, that Elliora's dreams of seeing stars meant she was a demon, possessed by the Night King himself. She told Elliora that seeing stars meant she was destined to kill, and since that day her mother ignored her as much as humanly possible.

Chapter One

Seven years earlier...

I'm dreaming of stars again. This time it's different though. Instead of vast, dark, emptiness, there is also a being. Well, a talking owl I suppose. At least that's what it looks like in my dream. It *feels* so real though. Like there is a being within that owl trying to speak to me. But the language . . . it is not of this world. I'm trying to listen, I really am. I'm trying *so* hard. But my eyes start to water, and my ears begin ringing. I know he is saying something important, just as I know this owl is actually a man. I can feel it in my bones. I can feel it in my soul. It feels like

I'm awake and trapped in a different world. A shiver runs through my body, and I look down at my arm, my pale skin bright against the darkness.

My arm has the cut I got yesterday and all my various freckles from too much time in the sun. The owl begins speaking louder now, bringing my attention back to him. I still don't know what this owl is saying, or why my dreams would happen in a language I don't know. All I know is that in this dream, I feel alive, and free. There's no trace of my harsh reality here, no weight of disappointment. No one looks at me with regret.

Suddenly the owl's blue-gray eyes pierce my own when he finally says, clear as day in my own human tongue, "Elliora, do not be afraid." Then he turns and flies off.

I wake abruptly, drenched in sweat, just as I always am after dreaming of stars. I can't tell anyone about my dreams; it would be a surefire way to never have anyone speak to me ever again. My sky blue sheets beneath me are so wet they are practically transparent. So I know I've been asleep for a while.

I get up and pad over to my tiny wooden desk, unlocking the drawer to pull out my secret journal. I write down all of the foreign words I can remember from the owl-being. *Am I spelling any of this right?* I have no idea, but I want to write down what I can before I forget. I sketch a picture of the owl and of all the stars I can remember seeing, all of their designs and patterns.

When I'm finished, I flip back through the notebook, and it's full of stars—endless stars. Some make different designs; some feel like they are calling to me. Hundreds of designs as I flip through, and yet I've never seen a single star in my life. I've never seen one, but I've dreamed of them for so long I feel like they are part of me.

There are also a few other pages with the same owl and his piercing blue-gray eyes. I don't know what any of it means. I probably shouldn't be writing it all down, creating evidence of my traitorous mind. It's so dangerous to do, but I just feel like I may need it someday. I can't explain why.

Here in Swaylin, it is always day. Twenty-four hours a day, all we have is the sun. There are never any clouds, except for once. One day, a couple weeks ago, I told my mother about my vivid dreams. The dreams that consumed my mind with stars, owls, and clouds. My mother was furious. She screamed at me, her face turning bright red with anger. I couldn't even hear her through the roaring in my ears and the tears that threatened to break free from my eyes. In that moment, a single gray cloud rolled across the sky.

People shouted as they hid in their shelters, praying to the Goddess Hemera, the Goddess of Day. My mother didn't seem to notice the cloud at first; she just kept yelling at me. Telling me I'd been possessed, that I was meant to kill.

I was so scared and confused. Why did my mother hate me so much? I can't imagine hating my own child. All of the other mothers in our town *loved* their children and would do anything for them. They protected them and cared for them, and here my mother was yelling that I was a demon on our front lawn.

When she finally did notice the cloud in the sky, she didn't seem surprised like everyone else in our town. There was no shriek; there was no running away. There was no scared mother telling her child to hide, or trying to protect me.

She stared at that cloud for what felt like the longest minute ever, turned back to me, and told me to "put the cloud away." She walked away with hatred in her eyes. I had so many questions, and not one of them answered.

My mother has been insane my entire life. They said that it happened after her journey to the Night Realm . . . that she left as a happy and caring teenager and returned to Day as a mad woman. So the day she told me I was a demon and that I needed to "put the cloud away" — everyone chalked her actions up to insanity. We haven't spoken about it since. Actually, we haven't spoken *at all.* Since that day, our interactions are nothing more than the equivalent of two ghosts passing each other in the halls. We live in the same home, partake in the same meals, but neither of us is eager to be present with the other for long.

She's not like the other moms. She has never asked about my school or asked how my day was. She was always just simply there, a wordless soul, drifting through life. She spends a lot of her time gardening in the vegetable farm she and my grandparents run. We produce about twenty-five percent of the produce for all of Swaylin.

Though I'm only twelve, when I'm not in school, I'm expected to be farming alongside them. Which isn't my idea of fun. I've never had a green thumb or been very good at gardening. However, I enjoy spending that time with my grandfather.

My grandfather lives with us, and is my best friend. He was never summoned to the Night Realm, so he is sharp and still has all his wits even in his old age, even despite losing my grandmother a year ago. My grandmother was never summoned either, so they were both shocked when my mom received her summons and even more alarmed when she came home pregnant and insane.

Grandfather is the only person in my life who seems to care about me. He takes care of me in ways my mother simply cannot. He tells me to keep my chin up; he asks how my day is. He's a simple man, with the same strawberry blond hair that my mother and I have, just peppered with gray. He wears a long-sleeved plaid shirt every day and a pair of jeans. His steel-toe farming boots might just be the only pair of shoes he owns. He's wrinkled more and more with his old age, but he still smiles like a young boy.

We spend a lot of time together farming. He tries to teach me everything he knows. I simply hate farming. For the rest of my family, farming comes easily, but not for me. I can't seem to keep a single plant alive. My grandfather keeps saying it just takes practice, but his eyes always have a hint of worry to them. He is probably afraid when he dies, this place will rot with me running it.

I look back down at the notebook I'm holding, full of stars and my secrets, when I hear someone else in the house wake up. I hide my notebook back in the hidden locked drawer and start getting ready for a long day in the sun.

Present Day

I stand at the edge of the ship admiring the Sea of Wanderers. Its beauty is truly breathtaking, and unlike anything I've ever seen. The sunlight dances across the sea, creating a gorgeous shade of blue as far as the eye can see. I've never had the chance to be at sea before, and as nervous as I am that I was summoned, I'm enjoying the wet sea breeze and salty air. I have never done well with the heat of the brutal sun in Swaylin, so the cool breeze is a welcome change for me. I startle when I hear the horn to signal that we are about to make the dark crossover. I was not expecting for us to reach this part of the journey for another few hours.

The crossing from Swaylin to the Night Realm takes four days by ship. However, the dark crossover only lasts two minutes.

For the duration of the dark crossover, everyone has to be secured in their quarters below deck. No one is allowed to witness the dark crossover except for the Captain. Even the ship's crew is to remain below deck for the full two minutes.

It feels ominous in that way, and I can't help but wonder *why* even the crew cannot witness it.

The instructions were very clear upon boarding, though. Stay below for two minutes or be killed instantly. So when the horn goes off again, I quickly make my way below deck, unwilling to take any chances. Honestly, I've been pretty happy at sea the last three days. I don't have to farm. I don't even have to be out in the sun if I don't want to. I can just stay below deck and read.

I'm rushing down the steps when just before I hit the bottom, my foot slips on the slick wet wooden floor. A man—no, a boy— rushes to the stairs and grabs my arm to keep me from falling.

"Thanks," I mumble, totally embarrassed that I almost ate it falling down a few steps. I step to the side while this boy still grips my arm, and the next thing I know the captain comes and slams down the hatch.

"I guess it's time," the mystery boy says with a grimace. "By the way, I'm Jaysen." He gives me a warm, friendly smile. I'm pretty sure I've never smiled like that in my entire life.

"Hi, Jaysen, I'm Elliora. I take it you were also summoned?" I try to smile at him and hope it doesn't look forced or awkward. I'm honestly just not used to smiling. And isn't that just so sad to say?

"Yes, and it sucks. I've been sick for the entirety of my time on this ship. But I'm glad I just ran into you. I'm already feeling a little better." He winks.

There is something odd about this whole interaction. Is he flirting with me? I truly don't know. My stomach is doing pancake flips and now *I* might be the one who is going to vomit.

I just smile at him and turn my head because I don't even know what to say. He slides his hand down my arm and holds my hand. Honestly, I don't pull away or try to stop it. We have to wait two minutes down here and it is oddly comforting to hold someone's hand while doing so. Everything goes silent, as if everyone is holding their breath.

I think to myself, *this has to be the longest two minutes of my life*, as my heart pounds in my chest. Jaysen squeezes my hand tighter. I try to look through the cracks of the floorboards, but all I see is black.

Another few moments pass, and there is a *thump-thump* from on deck, and then the crew begins making their way up the stairs again.

All of the summoned wait around for instruction, and when we finally realize there isn't going to be any, I let go of Jaysen's hand and take the first step up the stairs. I mean I'm sure I have the least to lose out of everyone down here.

I get to the top of the stairs, and my eyes start watering. It's so dark. Trying to adjust is almost painful for a minute. The sky is so black, and FULL of stars. They look exactly as I've imagined them in my dreams. I don't know why, but they are beautiful. They twinkle, glow, and look like magic. I cannot imagine why we've spent our entire existence living in fear of them. I cannot imagine why my mother thinks these are dead lives. Looking at them brings me a sense of joy I've never known, a sense of joy that doesn't feel real. The stars make it seem like anything is possible.

Jaysen walks up behind me and puts a hand on my back. Again, I don't stop him because it's comforting. I've never had someone care for me like this before. My grandfather 'cared' by just asking about my day, but never cared with a physical touch. He wouldn't hug or comfort me in any way. I think he was too afraid to, after the pain of losing my mother to insanity and my grandmother's death.

Jaysen finally speaks, "It's so...dark...and terrifying."

I look up, my eyes still watering, and whisper, "It's so...beautiful."

Chapter Two

THE INSTANT THE WORDS escaped my lips, I knew I'd made a huge mistake. Jaysen is from Swaylin, so of course, that was not the right thing to say to him.

I'm about to say something else—anything to seem remotely normal again—when a giant white barn owl slices through the sky with a piercing cry. It lands abruptly on the mass in front of us. It's strange, though, I've always seen white barn owls around, but as far as I know, they're not exactly common in Swaylin. I was also unsure if the Night Realm would have them as well.

This owl seems to be staring right at us. I look over at Jaysen beside me, who has gone stiff and pale. At this point, I might be looking at him with a hint of disgust because honestly, what "grown man" is afraid of a freaking owl?

I look back at the owl in front of me. It reminds me of the one from my dreams many years ago. There was an owl who spoke in an odd language to me, except this owl in front of me has different eyes—gold eyes. The one from my dream had blue-gray eyes that still haunt me to this day; they are forever engraved into my brain.

I spent hours in the library when I was fifteen trying to decipher the words the owl spoke. I know it's crazy to try and decipher gibberish from a dream, but I just couldn't let it go for some reason. I found some of the words in a banned book called *Old Language Magic*. Or at least, they seemed similar to the words I had scribbled down. It was pure dumb luck that I even found that banned book in the first place. I'd long since chalked it up to madness—mine, or maybe something I inherited from my mother. I hadn't thought about those dreams in over four years.

I glance back at the owl, and for a split second, I swear it gives me a curt nod before taking off again. I must be imagining things though—owls don't nod. Do they?

I watch it soar straight ahead, following the same path as our boat. When I turn back to Jaysen, he seems more like himself again. Calmer, and almost normal.

Jaysen says, "I don't think I can stomach it after the events of the last ten minutes, but would you like to get something to eat below deck?"

I look around at the dark night sky and sigh. I really want to stay up here with the stars. It's quite honestly the first time I've ever felt normal in my entire life. My skin is practically humming with joy and excitement.

However, I really could use a friend right now. I've spent most of my life alone, and with a whole new chapter about to begin, it would mean a lot to know someone when we get there. I look back at Jaysen and tell him, "I'd love to."

The food on board is actually surprisingly good. There's plenty of stew and oatmeal. They keep it simple, but it's far more satisfying than the endless vegetables I'm used to. Every meal has been delicious so far. I haven't asked what kind of meat is in the stew yet; part of me worries that once I know, I won't be able to eat it again.

Jaysen seems genuinely excited to have someone to share a meal with. We dig into tonight's stew, which is served with warm dinner rolls. While I find it comforting, he doesn't seem to enjoy it nearly as much. With every bite, his face twists into a subtle grimace, followed by a swallow so labored you can both see it in his throat and hear it in the silence between our bites.

Jaysen is all small talk and easy smiles, the kind of person who lights up a room even when he'd rather be anywhere else. In every way, he's my polar opposite. He radiates cheerfulness even while quietly loathing everything around him. I'm nervous about what will happen to him in the Night Realm. Will he return home to the family he clearly adores? He hasn't stopped talking about them for a good ten minutes now.

Jaysen is tall, with muscle in all the right places. His physique, all broad shoulders and thick arms, is a testament to what working a job in manual labor can do. Especially once I learned his family owns a farming equipment business. Honestly, it's a wonder we haven't crossed paths before this. He's from the other side of Swaylin, though, near the Fishing District. His older brother is the one who travels equipment to our side of Swaylin.

Jaysen has the kind of face and body most women would swoon over, and don't get me wrong, it's not like I haven't noticed. He has striking light golden hair and eyes that shift between green and blue depending on the light. His broad shoulders give him a strong presence, and every time he smiles, there is a playful twinkle that lights up his eyes. There's just something about him I can't quite put my finger on. Maybe it's how much he smiles, or how relentlessly positive he is. I know it sounds crazy to say that's a problem, but somehow, it feels off to me.

Jaysen and I finish up our stew and rolls. The chef on board comes by and asks me how it was. I tell him it was delicious as always, and he gives me a tight nod, as he does every night.

Jaysen looks up after the chef walks away. "Does he always ask you how the food was?"

"Yep! Every night so far." I force another smile, hoping it looks genuine. Honestly, I'm not used to working these facial muscles like this.

"Hm, that's odd. Well, let him know to try cooking something other than stew, would you? I'm terribly sick of it." Jaysen lets out a low chuckle that sends my stomach into a frenzy.

Good lord, I've never heard someone laugh so beautifully.

I smile at Jaysen. This time it at least feels a little more genuine. I let him know I'm getting tired and probably should retire for the evening. Jaysen smiles and offers to walk me to my quarters.

We step out of the dining hall, and honestly, I feel like I could live on this ship forever. While everyone else from Swaylin is battling seasickness, food fatigue, or waves of homesickness, I've found a surprising comfort here. My quiet days spent reading in my cozy little cabin have become some of the most peaceful and memorable moments I've ever experienced.

What does that say about me and my life before this?

We make our way down to my corridor. Jaysen tells me his room is one level just below. When we reach my door, I catch myself holding my breath. I've never really dated before. I've never really had a man interested in me, romantically. The boys I'd known were only interested in one thing, and when they got it they disappeared. Could Jaysen actually be interested in more? Could that be what's happening now?

Jaysen looks down at me in the narrow corridor, and I can see in his eyes that he wants something more than I'm ready for. Am I scared because I just met him? Or because those might really be his intentions? Despite my roller-coaster of emotions, it is more unsettling not knowing what to expect when we get to the Night Realm. I need someone. Someone to be on this journey with. I do not want to be alone.

On a quick impulse, I rise onto my toes and press a gentle kiss to his lips.

"Thank you for the lovely company today. See you to-morrow," I whisper.

I hurry into my tiny cabin before I can process what happened or catch a glimpse of his reaction, quickly shutting the door behind me.

As I grin, thinking of his reaction, I turn to face my "room." We were only allowed a single small bag they provided us with to take to the Night Realm. I only brought enough clothing for five days, because I wanted to fit as many of my books as I could. I hope they have some kind of washing system when we arrive, or I might be wearing some very worn and dirty clothes.

The space they provide us with is incredibly cramped. It's just enough to fit a narrow cot pressed against the wall. There is barely enough room for anything else, other than the small lamp perched on a slender, barely-there ledge. I'm not sure how some of the males like Jaysen are faring. My cot is barely big enough for me, and I'm only 5'2". I can't imagine being around 6' and trying to squeeze on this cot every night.

There is a single, tiny porthole, barely big enough to peek through, its faint light always dimmed by a threadbare, shadowy curtain that hangs limply, casting a muted gloom over the space. I've had it closed for the past three nights, as we sailed through the Day Realm.

Now, though, I want it open. As I open it I am only met with darkness. Though I am too far down to see the brighter stars above I can still see some faint ones in the distance that make my heart skip a beat.

I strip off today's clothes, find my toothbrush, and brush my teeth with a bottle of water I've been storing under my cot and a bowl I snuck out of the dining room on the first day. I rinse and spit into the bowl, and put it all back in place.

I climb into my cot, clutching my book, and smile up at the ceiling. The porthole casts a soft glow from distant stars, gently illuminating my tiny space. Around me, the cramped quarters buzz with noise, but despite the chaos, I feel a quiet happiness settle in. It's strange, today I realized something: I don't think I've ever truly felt happiness before.

My skin gets a tingly feeling, and when I look down, my freckles are almost glowing. Like . . . stars.

Chapter Three

I step into the dining room for breakfast and immediately feel a slight dizziness wash over me as I take in the bustling scene. Everyone is in a flurry of activity, buzzing with anticipation for our expected arrival to the Night Realm later this evening. The temperature has dropped a lot since we made the dark crossing, so I'm wearing the one and only coat I brought with me for the journey. It's a knee-length black trench coat with plenty of pockets. I thought it might come in handy when we arrive in the Night Realm.

Jaysen starts frantically waving at me across the small dining room. He is sitting off to the right with another guy.

I wave back and gesture that I'm going to grab food first. Jaysen does a ridiculous thumbs-up back to me.

I'm heading toward the breakfast buffet when the same chef comes over with a plate of food. He's a short man who walks with a limp. He has kind eyes, or at least that is what my grandmother would say. His gray eyes hold mine as he smiles wide. His smile has one tooth missing. "Mornin', I got this special for you." He hands me the plate quickly and scurries away.

I look down at the plate full of oatmeal, fruit, and a bread roll. Huh, that was a really odd thing for him to do. I shrug, take the plate anyway, and head for Jaysen.

Jaysen and the guy next to him exchange a curious look. Jaysen looks back at me as I'm sitting down, and says "I don't think you should eat that . . ."

I glance up at him. "Why not?"

"It might be poisoned," Jaysen whispers across the table.

"Oh nonsense! I'm sure it's fine." I start eating and rip apart the roll to dip in my oatmeal. It's not that I'm too trusting, it's that I don't care. It is a hard realization to have at nineteen, that I truly wouldn't care if my food was poisoned. What am I really living for anyways?

Jaysen scrunches his nose and whispers again, "Do you actually like this stuff?"

I nod, and Jaysen flinches like he is physically hurt by my words.

"Have you not had good food before?!" Jaysen and the mystery guy start laughing together.

I turn to his friend after his reaction to Jaysen's question. He looks oddly similar to Jaysen. They are both tall, both incredibly tan, and packed with muscles. Jaysen's golden blond hair is on the darker side of blond, where this new mystery guy has bright blond hair, almost white. Honestly, it's perfect for Swaylin. I'm sure there are some girls back in Swaylin very upset over his summoning. Both boys have bright white smiles, matching greenish-blue eyes, and freckles sprinkled across their noses. Jaysen has dimples that are always visible, though, thanks to his naturally cheerful demeanor.

I extend my hand. "Hi, I'm Elliora." I force another smile, but inside, I wrestle with doubt. Will I have to keep pretending forever, or will a genuine smile ever come effortlessly?

Jaysen's friend takes my hand in a firm handshake and says, "Hey, I'm Brockcorigan, but my friends call me Brock!"

"Nice to meet you," I respond. I lower my face toward my food and start shoveling it in, silently hoping they'll carry on their conversation from before I arrived.

To my pleasant surprise, it works, and they do. Jaysen and Brock continue talking about what they think we are being summoned for, how long we might be away, what the Night Realm might be like, and more.

I finish my meal and wipe down my area, making sure everything is tidy. Carrying my tray, I walk over to the trash and the bin for dirty dishes. Just as I toss the last item away, the chef approaches me once again and says, "May I speak with you for a second, Miss Elliora?"

I glance back at Jaysen and Brock, but they're not watching. Turning to the chef, I give a quick nod. He starts walking, and I hurry after him down the hall that leads to the kitchen.

Once we're in the hallway, out of sight, the chef turns to face me. "My name is Taterfall, you can call me Tate. I'm a friend of your dad's."

The room seems to tilt for a second, his words ringing in my ears. I blink, completely caught off guard. "I'm sorry—did you just say my *dad's*?"

"Yeah, I just didn't want you to think I was some weirdo lurking around, handing you food." He pauses, as if there's more he wants to say but isn't sure how.

"Uhm, okay. Who exactly is my dad?" I lower my voice to a whisper, hesitant to speak any louder. I'd rather not broadcast the fact that my father isn't from Swaylin. Not that it's much of a secret. I'm sure most people in town have probably already guessed, or at least suspect it.

"I'm not at liberty to say quite yet. Your father was rather specific about not revealing his true identity, I think he wants to do it himself . . ." He pauses.

I'm thoroughly confused now. "Okay. Could you maybe not share this with anyone on the ship? This isn't exactly the kind of information I need people to have right now."

"Oh, of course, I would never, I just need you to know, sorry, I uhh . . . need to start working on lunch, I just wanted to make sure you knew I could be trusted." He then proceeds to quickly walk off towards the sink. Going about his business like he didn't just drop a bombshell on me.

Trusted? This news honestly makes me trust him . . . less?

I stand in the hallway in a state of shock. I've always known my dad was in the Night Realm, but when I received the summons, I never imagined I'd actually have the chance to meet him. My mother hadn't been very far along when she came back to Swaylin. My grandparents even tried to deny he was from the Night Realm at one point when I was little, but it was a lost cause. I knew the truth all along, and I was almost certain he didn't even know I existed...

I feel like my world has tilted off its axis. The ground seems to sway beneath me, and my vision blurs at the edges. I stumble back, catching myself against the wall, my hands braced on my knees as I struggle to steady my breath. For a moment, everything spins. But after a few deep, deliberate breaths, the haze begins to lift. I pull myself upright, slowly reclaiming my composure.

I walk back into the dining hall. I'm doing everything I can to keep one foot in front of the other. Jaysen and Brock come rushing over. "Are you okay?" Jaysen looks completely beside himself.

"I'm fine, I didn't sleep much last night." Which is a total lie. "I think I'm going to rest before we arrive in the Night Realm. Since we aren't really sure what to expect."

Jaysen continues looking extremely concerned, but says, "Sure, that's probably a good idea, I'll walk you to your quarters." He turns to Brock. "Be back soon." Brock nods and we start walking out of the dining hall.

Brock shouts, "Feel better, Elliora, see you when we are back on land!"

I turn around and wave at him as we head out of the hall.

We are in my corridor again, heading for my room. This time, Jaysen is confident enough to hold my hand the whole way.

We get to my cabin, and he leans down and kisses my forehead. "I know we just met Elliora, but I really like you already."

I catch myself before rolling my eyes. Does he really mean that?

"Get some rest, I'll see you on the other side." He smiles, squeezes my hand, and walks off.

I know people believe in "love at first sight" "soulmates" and even "mates" in some realms. I can't help but think, though, that we . . . aren't. I don't feel any kind of connection with him. I just feel the need to have some kind of companionship while going into a new world.

I walk through the door and into my cabin. I guess I'm stuck in here now at least for a couple hours, although I don't mind. I walk to the porthole . . . it's still night. I really can't believe it. The stars are the prettiest shade of purple now.

Staring up at the stars, my mind drifts over the last twenty-four hours. I'm meeting new people, making new connections that will hopefully be friends I can rely on, and then I got news that shook me to my core. Not only does my dad know I exist, but he knows I'm on my way . . . to him. Suddenly, I feel a new sense of purpose stirring inside me. At the very least, I need to see what he looks like.

I honestly could stand here all day and admire these stars. I look down at my freckles, but they aren't glowing. Maybe I imagined that last night. A cool chill runs down my spine, the hairs on my arms prickling as an owl's piercing cry echoes in the distance. I peer through the porthole, and see him—the same golden eyes from yesterday.

Chapter Four

AT SOME POINT DURING my hiding and reading, I must've actually dozed off. I awake to loud banging and shouting. I fly out of my bed and rush to my door, swinging it open in a hurry. There is a man in all black walking up and down the hall yelling "ONE HOUR TILL DOCKING, PACK UP YOUR SHIT, ONE HOUR!"

Chaos erupts in the cabins around me—people are crying, screaming, frantically shoving their belongings into bags. Luckily, I never really "unpacked" so I put my current book in my bag. With my coat now on, there's a bit of space left in my bag, just enough to shove in the bowl I stole—I might need it, wherever we're headed.

I stare at the bowl sitting in my bag for a long minute. I thought the chef kept talking to me because he knew I stole this bowl, but the reality was way worse . . . He knows my *dad*.

It's strange—I've spent my whole life completely oblivious. My mother and grandfather never uttered a word about him. It wasn't until I learned about the "birds and the bees" that I realized I *must* have a dad out there somewhere. My grandmother once mentioned something about my dad being in the Night Realm before she passed, but my grandfather shushed her and said we don't speak of such things.

I wish I knew something, and I mean *anything*. Will I see him? Will he come for me? I wonder if he ever even wanted to meet me. What would he have done if I had never been summoned? Or better yet, is he the reason *why* I was summoned?

I sling my bag over my shoulder and take one last look at my cramped little cabin. Surprisingly, I'm going to miss it. Life on the ship grew on me—I actually enjoyed it. Now that I know that, maybe one day I'll join the crew of a boat like this for real. It sounds a whole lot better than a future in farming.

I turn and head up the stairs to the deck. Chaos greets me—passengers and crew scramble in a frenzy, rushing to finish last-minute tasks before we dock. I still can't see the port, but in this darkness, it might be closer than it seems.

While I was napping, I missed lunch, so my stomach begins to growl. I turn my back to the sea and spot Jaysen walking straight toward me, a small brown bag in his hand.

"That weird chef guy told me to give this to you since you missed lunch." He sighs. "I would tell you not to eat it again, but you're probably hungry..."

"I'm starving, so I'm eating it . . ." I say with a smile, "poisoned or not"

He gives me a tight smile in return, and we look out at the sea together. I feel so peaceful. We didn't live near the ocean in Swaylin. I can't help but wonder how different life would've been if I had felt this kind of peace a decade sooner.

I quickly eat the sandwich from the bag, and wish there was another. I truly did enjoy the food on board.

Jaysen whispers, "We should be there soon."

Brock comes behind from out of nowhere. "Captain just told a group of crew members we would be there in ten minutes." He smiles at me. "Elliora, how are you feeling?"

"So much better, I took a nap, and now that I've eaten this sandwich, I'm ready for anything." I grin at him.

Suddenly, there are gasps and whispers across the ship. Someone shouts, "There it is! I can't believe it!"

I turn to look and see what everyone is pointing at, and I'm at a loss for words. It's... incredible. Before us stretches the bustling dock, alive with the faint hum of activity under the night sky. Beyond it rises a thriving cityscape, a mosaic of towering glass skyscrapers that shimmer like giants made of crystal. Their reflective surfaces catch the glow of countless purple stars scattered across the velvet darkness above, casting a mesmerizing celestial dance of light.

Closer to the water's edge, clusters of smaller glass buildings mingle with cozy, warmly lit houses, their windows flickering like fireflies in the night. In the distance, framing the valley's edges, majestic snow-capped mountains stand sentinel—silent, timeless giants bathed in soft starlight.

It seems that anything that could safely be crafted from glass has been, shimmering with translucent elegance. Even the port is a gleaming wonder of glasswork, crowned by a sparkling archway and a luminous sign that twinkle like jewels in the night. "City of Canopus" the sign reads.

The whole view is absolutely breathtaking. I can't help but wonder how many cities there are in the Night Realm, and which one my dad might be in. Is he here, in the city of Canopus?

Jaysen grabs my hand. "It looks terrifying."

At this moment, I can't help but wonder if all my dreams have meant more. Was my mother right when she called me a Night Demon? Am I destined to kill? Because right now, Jaysen and I are looking at the same view. However, I'm the only one who thinks it's the most beautiful place I've ever seen.

Chapter Five

THE REST OF THE journey to the dock is quiet. A nervous energy crackles in the air. It seems like everyone from Swaylin is too scared to speak. Only the crew seems to understand what's coming next. Our dark ship cuts silently through the water toward the glowing port, its shimmering lights casting long reflections on the water. As we draw nearer, the crew springs into action, methodically beginning the precise dance of docking procedures with quiet, practiced urgency.

Our group of summoned Swaylinis stays on deck awaiting our orders. They move the gangplank into position as a tall man dressed in all black climbs aboard. His green eyes immediately capture my attention. They shimmer like rare gemstones, mysterious and otherworldly, as if holding ancient secrets. He radiates power while his black hair flows in the ocean breeze. His pale skin speaks of a life untouched by the sun's harsh rays—something I find myself quietly envying. At his side hangs an immaculate sword, its polished blade gleaming softly in the light. The handle is intricately carved, curling into the shape of a majestic dragon, its fierce eyes seeming to hold a silent power.

I can't shake the thought that dragons might actually exist in a place like this. Here, where the air hums with magic and possibility, it feels like anything, no matter how fantastical, could come to life.

As soon as this powerful stranger is on board, he makes his way to the steps leading to the Captain's Quarters, and turns to face us all. "Welcome to the Night Realm." He clears his throat once before continuing, "I know you've had a long journey, and I'm sure you have many questions. We promise we will get to them, but we want you to rest and find your place in our home first. My staff will be on board shortly to escort you to your new rooms, which are straight ahead in the Orion Palace." He then gestures to the furthest, and the tallest, glass buildings off in the distance.

"We will get you all fed, rested, and clean before meeting tomorrow morning for our very first training session. If you have any questions about your beds, food, or anything of that nature—my staff will be happy to answer them." As he finishes his speech, the members of his staff come onto the ship. He has one staff member for every person summoned. He must truly be a man of great influence to command so many staff members.

Just then, a brave Swaylini shouts from across the deck, "Sir, what is your name?"

The powerful man smiles. "I'm King Canis, King of the Night Realm, and Captain of the Ursa Major Navy," and with that, he comes down the steps and takes off down the gangplank. He doesn't even glance back.

The staff begin moving and shouting to find their assigned Swaylini. A beautiful woman dressed in a black and silver blouse with slick black leather pants comes up to me. She has two swords strapped across her back, along with twin daggers on each hip. Glancing down, I see there is at least one more weapon hiding in her boot. Her long, raven-black hair is braided gracefully over one shoulder, cascading nearly to her hip. Her eyes, a striking shade of green, gleam with quiet intensity. I glance around. It seems like everyone in the Night Realm has green or blue eyes that glow in the starlight.

The mystery woman smiles at me. "Are you Elliora Polaris?"

"Yep, that's me." I let go of Jaysen's hand. I almost forgot he was even holding my hand. The woman reaches out to grab my bag from me.

I shake my head. "I'll carry it."

"Suit yourself, but it's a mile walk to the palace." She smiles and starts walking off.

I look over at Jaysen, and repeat his phrase from earlier, "See you on the other side?"

Jaysen smiles. "I hope so." He grabs my hand again, gives it a squeeze, and then lifts it to his lips and presses a kiss to it.

I follow the woman carefully down the gangplank, and we begin to stroll through a charming cobblestone village square, where every building seems to mirror the stars above. I can't quite tell what creates the effect, whether it's some subtle shimmer in the stone or a paint crafted to make the walls softly glow.

It's mid-afternoon, from what I can guess, and the village is quiet. Everyone seems to be sitting out on their porches or balconies watching us arrive.

"Is it always this quiet in this village?" I ask the woman escorting me.

"No, it's usually bustling and full of music. Several street performers, shops are busy, people are working, trolleys are running. However, on this day each year, everyone takes time off to wait for the arrival of the summoned." She glances over her shoulder at me. "Are you sure you don't want me to carry your bag? We are going to begin our uphill part of the journey."

I look up at the hill ahead. We've got about at least another half mile or more that is straight uphill to the palace. It's not a steep incline, though. "I think I can handle it."

"Alright then." She keeps walking at a steady pace as we start our slow incline uphill. I don't bother talking anymore. There is just no point, so I take in the sights around me. It feels as though we are completely surrounded in every direction by snowcapped mountains. I can't help but wonder if it is still Night Realm on the other side. I also can't help but wonder where my father resides and how my mother managed to even find him while she was here.

As if this mystery woman can sense my thoughts, she says, "To the north are the Cassiopeian Mountains. You are forbidden to go north, *ever*. Even I cannot travel north. To the south are the Pleiades Mountains, you are welcome to travel south eventually, should you find a reason." She pauses and looks over her shoulder at me, in what I assume is an attempt to make sure I'm actually listening. "When we are not training, you are welcome to move around as you see fit, as long as you return in time for the next training session."

I nod my head.

We are almost to the palace when she turns and stops so fast I barely have time to stop myself. "I highly recommend never traveling alone. If I am not busy, I am happy to accompany you anywhere you want. I do have other jobs aside from catering to you, but as of right now, *you* are my number one priority. Do not get me in trouble."

I nod my head again.

"Good, let's get you to your room for a bath." And with that we continue on our way. We walk straight to the palace, and eventually arrive at the front doors. The massive arched double doors of gleaming glass swing open, revealing a grand foyer that takes my breath away. At its center stands a colossal glass desk, where four people work with intense focus. Staff rush past in a flurry of purposeful motion, their footsteps echoing through the vast space. The palace stands at least ten stories high; I tilt my head back to admire a soaring glass ceiling, where purple stars shimmer softly against the twilight sky above. Beneath my feet, the black marble floor sparkles delicately, mirroring the night sky in a shimmering dance of light. Overwhelmed, I struggle to absorb the sheer magnificence surrounding me.

"Come with me," says the dark-haired woman, who has yet to mention her name to me.

We approach one of the two elaborate staircases flanking the grand foyer and ascend the one on the left. Reaching the second floor, we head toward a sleek elevator nestled at the center—directly behind the enormous glass desk below. There are a few other people in the elevator with us as she presses a button for floor eleven, the top floor, and swipes a card for access.

A couple of the other staff members whisper amongst themselves, but it's too quiet for me to hear what they are saying. We stop along floors four, eight, and nine for the others to exit before it's just the two of us heading up to floor eleven. As the elevator doors open, I follow her into the hallway, where open glass railings offer a clear view down to all the floors below. Each level is lined with similar glass barriers, forming sharp rectangular outlines, while the floors alternate between deep purple and black hues. We round the first corner, and she stops in front of a door marked with the number 1111.

She again swipes the card, and opens the door to let me in. I glance back down to the other floors. They are full of my fellow summoned passengers and their escorts. I look around floor eleven, but I only see one other passenger from my ship on the opposite side. I take a deep breath to calm my nerves, and turn back around to head into the room.

The sight truly leaves me speechless.

The palace's glass ceiling extends into my room, the purple stars now shifting softly to a shimmering blue-gold hue. To the left, a private bathing room awaits, while a cozy sitting area rests to the right. Straight ahead, a hallway leads to the bedroom. I step inside to find a lavish four-poster bed crafted entirely from gleaming silver. Its side rails and posts are intricately etched with delicate stars, but the centerpiece is the headboard—a majestic owl with wings spread wide in a graceful, protective embrace. I get goosebumps looking at it. Why have owls followed me my whole life?

I turn back to look at the dark-haired woman as she begins to speak. "My name is Ataksak. If you need anything at all during your time here, just ask. There is a bath and a shower in your bathing room."

"A shower?" I ask.

"Ah, yes, I forgot Swaylin is not blessed with them yet. The water falls from above to clean yourself off. Think of it like a waterfall? There are soaps in there as well." She glances at something attached to her wrist. "I have to be somewhere in two minutes. Bathe, rest, and make yourself comfortable. Here is your access card; it only works for this room. You will need it for room entry and the elevator. I will come get you in an hour for dinner." And with that, she hands me the silver sparkling card, turns on her heel and leaves the room quickly.

The door clicks shut behind her, and I stand frozen, staring at it for a long moment. Slowly, I circle around to the other side of the bed. There, a vast window stretches from floor to ceiling, framing a breathtaking view of the snowcapped mountains beyond. I'm staring out the window, thinking of all the things I've been told about the Night Realm. The summoning is dreaded; people come home insane, some not at all, but why do I feel like I'm the luckiest girl in the world for being here right now?

Chapter Six

I've just taken my first shower ever, and it was magical. I've washed my clothes in the bathtub, brushed my teeth, hung my clothes to dry on the shower rail, and now I'm brushing my hair. The bathroom has several drawers, which I open to find extra soaps, fresh towels, and a variety of essentials. To my surprise, there are even some makeup products neatly tucked inside. I've never been permitted to wear makeup in Swaylin due to our farming culture and the fact that my family could never afford it.

I look at the brushes and products, and start to play with them. I try on what I believe is meant for my lips and paint them a beautiful shade of red. I continue looking through the products and swipe some black products on my eyelashes. I've seen enough beautiful women in my life to know those two things. However, I have no idea what the rest of it does, or where to put it on my face.

I look at myself in the mirror. Wow, what a difference a shower and a tiny bit of makeup make. I feel like I belong here.

The ceiling above is glass as well, even in the bathroom. The stars now seem to glow a shimmering, silvery white. I walk out of the bathroom with the towel still wrapped tightly around me. There is a dresser in the bedroom. I open one of the drawers to find clothes. I don't know if they are meant for me? I hold up the shirt. It sure seems like it would fit great, and since my clothes are likely still damp, I slide the shirt on over my head.

It fits perfectly, and now I'm slightly creeped out. Did they know my size prior to my arrival?

I rummage through the drawers and find a pair of black pants. I slide them on, and again, they are a perfect fit. I lie back on my new bed and gaze up at the stars. A quiet tune escapes my lips, a song my mother used to hum to herself when I was a child. Just as the melody takes shape, a tingling sensation creeps across my skin. I glance down. My freckles are glowing again.

I leap to my feet and rush to the bathroom mirror. The freckles on my face are glowing, pulsing faintly like tiny stars. Heart pounding, I shut my eyes and draw in a deep breath. When I open them again, the glow has vanished. There is a swift knock on my door when I hear Ataksak enter the room.

"Elliora, are you ready for dinner?" she yells through the bathroom door.

"Yep, be right out." I glance at myself again; the glowing seems to have stopped. It's a relief . . . unless I'm actually losing my mind. Either way, I'm not ready to tell anyone about this, at least not yet.

I head out of the bathroom and ask Ataksak if there are extra coats anywhere, as mine is still damp from washing. She walks over to a cabinet I hadn't noticed in the sitting area and pulls out a coat. I'm not even surprised to see that, once again, it's a perfect fit.

We head down the elevators to the fifth floor. Ataksak tells me this is where the dining hall and kitchen are located. There is an hour long breakfast buffet in the morning, but if you miss it you are, as she says, "Shit outta luck." There is a three hour window for lunch. Lunch has a buffet and a menu to order from. Dinner is served promptly every day at the same time. If you are not seated in the first five minutes, you have to head to floor one to get something from a small cafe located there.

I keep repeating this to myself. This is nothing like the free-for-all I've known my whole life. Back then, meals were scattered, unstructured. My mother never sat down to eat with me, as we were always on different rhythms. Every now and then, if our schedules happened to align, my grandfather would join me for lunch, but those moments were rare.

Ataksak stops at the doors to the dining hall. She turns to me and says, "You will find me here when you are done with your meal. Enjoy!" She turns and briskly walks away.

I enter the dining hall and look around, and immediately my eyes find Jaysen's. I smile, and head his way. Of course, he has Brock sitting to his left, so I take a seat across the table from him. He reaches his hand across the table and takes my hand in his. "You look beautiful, Elliora, the Night Realm suits you. How was your hour? How was your room?"

I take a minute to wonder if I should speak the truth or conceal my true feelings. I opt for truth. "It's honestly beautiful. The shower was magical. I feel so . . . clean"

He smiles at me. "I'm glad! My shower was quite rushed. There was a large line for it on the eighth floor. What floor are you on? I didn't see you."

I can feel heat creeping up my face as I realize we don't all have the same accommodations. I wonder how they chose who got what. I'm just a nobody from a farming village in Swaylin. Why would I have a private bathroom when Jaysen has to share?

I stumble over my words. "I, uh, was placed, uhm . . . on floor eleven."

"Wow! I haven't heard anyone else say they were up that high! Must be why that floor had no line for the shower."

I don't bother telling him I have my own. I feel like I'll save that information for another time. The dining hall doors remain wide open when a sudden, piercing cry slices through the chatter, freezing every voice in the room. I turn toward the entrance just as a massive white owl sweeps inside, its wings whispering against the air. It glides with eerie grace before landing on a chair near the front, its golden eyes scanning the silent crowd.

A bell sounds from the kitchen, and staff in black aprons start coming through the kitchen doors with platters.

Staff begin placing elegant platters of food before each of us, the aromas rich and inviting. Yet the other summoned hesitate, eyeing their meals with suspicion and unease.

It strikes me as unlikely, they've brought us this far; poisoning us now would be a waste of effort.

I pick up my fork and start eating. Nearby, a woman moves gracefully through the room with a decanter of wine. She pauses by my side, raising an eyebrow in a silent offer. I nod in return, signaling that I'll have some.

The food is exquisite, each bite bursting with flavor. The wine is smooth and rich. This meal might be the best thing I've ever tasted. Honestly, I could get used to a life this lavish. I've spent my whole life sweating on a farm, burning more calories under the sun than I ever managed to replace. To eat like this, without worry or restraint... I could do it forever.

The rest of the meal is fine. I enjoy chatting with Jaysen and Brock. Even though it's obvious they're far more interested in my body than my mind, I don't let it show. It's clear we're not alike, our personalities don't align, but I play along. I still need allies for whatever lies ahead. More than that, I need to stay grounded, to keep my sanity intact. And that means keeping people close, even if the connection is shallow.

We make small talk about our lives in Swaylin. I definitely glamorize mine to sound a bit more interesting. Towards the end of our meal, Jaysen grabs my hand from across the table again. As soon as he does, there is a loud boom.

I glance over to where the owl was perched.

There is no longer an owl.

There is a man.

Holy shit, there is a man there.

The man's gaze pins me in place. A prickling sensation creeps across my skin, and I lower my eyes—paranoid that my freckles might start glowing again.

Are others feeling this too? What's happening to me? Is this the same madness that broke my mother?

My thoughts spiral out of control. My heart pounds loudly in my chest, and a cold sweat forms on my skin. Am I about to pass out?

I let go of Jaysen's hand, keep my eyes down at the table, and finish up my food. After a few bites, I risk a peek at Jaysen, who is still staring with his jaw practically on the floor, looking at this owl-man, man-owl? I don't even know. That man has to be what was once an owl? Right? *RIGHT*?

I can't even process what is happening right now. I take a drink of wine as the woman serving wine comes around again.

"Excuse me, may I have some more?"

She smiles and pours more into my cup. I glance around. People are finishing up their food, and a few people are retreating back out of the dining hall doors. I stand up suddenly and look at Jaysen. I have to let out a fake cough to even get his attention. He and Brock are completely mesmerized by the owl guy, and I can't say I blame them. He is quite possibly the most gorgeous human I've ever seen, but I am currently avoiding eye contact.

"I'm going to retire for the evening." I look at Jaysen and then Brock. "Thank you for another lovely meal together."

I start to head out when Jaysen comes up behind me. He grabs my hand, and I turn to look up at him. He's got dreamy eyes, I will say that.

"Elliora, why don't I walk you to your room? We can continue talking." He offers me what I can only guess is his "seductive smile," the same one he probably flashes at women all the time. Somehow, it feels oddly rehearsed, like a performance rather than genuine.

Suddenly, it hits me: I'm not the first. He's done this before, countless times, and I'm just the fool who's never had a man look at her like this.

I feel caught in a vicious cycle. On one hand, I need allies. I still don't know what tomorrow will bring. But on the other hand, I'm realizing I don't feel the same way about

Jaysen. It's becoming painfully clear that's the only way he sees me.

I'm trying to figure out how to tell him that I don't know the rules in this new home, and trying to figure out how to escape this situation. When suddenly, a strong grip pulls me into their body. I turn around to find the owl-man behind me, pulling me into him like we've known each other forever.

"I will make sure she gets to her quarters safely, goodnight," owl-man says to Jaysen, dismissing him quickly. He spins around, pulling me along effortlessly, whisking me away like a damn knight in shining armor.

Before I can think, speak, or even process how my life shifted from farming in Swaylin to this moment in just five days, we're already out of the dining hall doors

As we exit, Ataksak comes up as promised. She glances between owl-man and me and smiles.

"I see you've made a new friend, Elliora." She smirks at me.

Owl-Man lets out a low grumble. "I will make sure Elliora makes it to her quarters. Goodnight, Atta."

I raise my eyebrows at Ataksak. "Atta, huh?"

She laughs. "We aren't that close yet. Maybe tomorrow. Goodnight, Elliora, see you in the morning." She winks and heads off in the opposite direction while whistling a tune.

Owl-man grabs my hand and leads me with unwavering purpose. His grip is firm, his pace unrelenting. Without hesitation, he pushes past the line at the elevators, slipping inside just as the doors begin to open. Before anyone can protest, he shuts the doors behind us. He presses the button for the eleventh floor and swipes a sleek, black card against the panel—smooth, practiced, like he's done this a hundred times before.

The elevator starts heading up.

I glance over at him, and looking at him is a mistake.

This man is, without a doubt, the sexiest person I've ever laid eyes on. His eyes are owl-like in the most mesmerizing way. They are a striking shade of gold, intense and unblinking. His hair is a sleek silver-gray, tousled just enough to look effortlessly perfect. A scatter of freckles dances across his cheekbones. They are star-like, as if the night sky has kissed his skin. He towers over me, easily a foot taller, and every inch of him is wrapped in fitted black clothing that clings to his frame in all the right places. There's no question he's built beneath it. Just above his collar, a hint of a tattoo teases the edge of his neckline, barely visible but impossible to ignore.

I start to admire his chiseled jawline when I realize I'm ogling.

Gods, when have I *ever* ogled over a man like this? What is wrong with me? I stare ahead at the elevator door in front of me. It dings open just in time to break my intrusive thoughts about this owl-man. He grabs my hand again and begins pulling me down the hall.

I'm desperate to start a conversation.

"Where does the staff sleep?" I ask.

He glances over at me. "There are various staff members on every floor, and some live out in the servant's house in the back of the palace."

We get to my door, and he swipes his black card again. The door opens, and he shoves me inside and follows me in.

The door closes behind him.

"Uhm, can I help you? I didn't really expect you to just waltz into my room? Is this some kind of staff check or protocol?" I question.

"No, Elliora, I must be quick, I really shouldn't be in here." He lets out a heavy sigh. "You need to hide your magic as long as possible."

I'm completely confused and stunned at this point. "I'm sorry, *my magic?*"

He sighs again as if this is a totally normal conversation and not the weirdest thing I've ever experienced.

"Yes, your glowing freckles indicate that you have magic. The training sessions you will be summoned to are designated to find those with magic. You need to hide it as long as you possibly can," he demands.

I stumble over my thoughts, and I can't seem to find the words, so I just repeat again, "Magic?"

"Yes, you wouldn't have known about it in Swaylin, due to the curse. Here, though, they already assume you might have the magic, that's why you were put on the highest floor. To be closer to the stars." He gestures up at the glass ceiling above.

"You—they—think *I'm* magic?" I burst out laughing. I don't know why, maybe it's the shock, or maybe I'm slowly losing my mind like my mother, but I genuinely can't stop laughing.

I finally catch my breath, and owl-man is staring at me. "Are you quite finished?" His arms are crossed over his chest, and he is clearly angry with me. I want to laugh again. He is being completely ridiculous, but I decide against it.

"You will feel it pulsing beneath your skin in training sessions, do whatever you can to not let it show. Bite your tongue, think of sunlight, think negative thoughts. Your happiness will only bring it out more, and if you can—be tired, don't sleep. Rest, and a full stomach will only make your magic stronger. That's why you stay here and are fed as you are."

There is a long pause as he stares blankly at me.

"I have to go, I will return to you tomorrow after training." He starts to turn and head out the door.

"Wait, who are you?" I whisper, "and how do I know I can trust you?"

He smiles, and my knees practically buckle at the sight. His brooding anger was sexy, but damn, that smile could drop panties for sure.

"My name is Pollux, and I don't have anything to prove. You should trust me, just . . . listen to your heart." With that, he turns and walks away, disappearing down the hallway. The door clicks softly shut behind him.

Chapter Seven

I REPLAY THE EVENING'S events over and over in my mind as I lie back in the most luxurious bed I've ever touched. The silk sheets cocoon me, and the plush mattress cradles my body like a cloud. Above me, the night sky stretches endlessly, framed by a glass ceiling that still feels too magical to be real. Stars shimmer overhead, silent and distant, and I can't help but stare.

I know I should be scared, or confused, at the very least. Everything about this place is unfamiliar. I have no idea what tomorrow will bring, or even what this all *means*. But strangely, I feel calm.

I'm the cleanest I've ever been, my skin still tingling slightly from the warmth of another luxurious shower and the scent of fresh, expensive soaps. My stomach is full of the most delicious food I've tasted in . . . maybe ever. Every part of me feels cared for, down to the soft fabric of the clothes I've been given. I feel, oddly, like a princess.

Uncertainty still hangs in the air, but for now, wrapped in warmth and starlight, I let myself feel peace.

I'm holding a book in front of my face, but I'm not really reading it. Honestly, right now I am wishing I had stolen some kind of book about the Night Realm from the restricted section of the Swaylini Library. This fictional book about characters falling in love is doing me absolutely no good right now.

As I lay in this bed and stare up at what feels like close to a million stars, I start to wonder about Pollux. There's something slightly off about him, something I can't quite place. Yet, for some reason, I feel like I should trust him.

And magic? He actually used the word *magic*? I only have the vaguest idea what that even means, and most of it comes from creepy campfire stories in Swaylin. I thought they were old made-up tales to scare kids into behaving better.

Honestly, I still think they are? But the glowing freckles . . . was I just imagining that? I'm starting to see why my mother went mad in this place. When truth and reality blur, sanity doesn't stand a chance.

I must've fallen asleep somewhere between my frantic thoughts and the madness of the night. I'm jolted awake by a sudden pounding on the door, and seconds later, Ataksak bursts in, striding into the room like she owns the place.

She is dressed much like the day before, in sleek, form-fitting black clothes, her hair pulled back into two neat braids today.

"Good day, sunshine," she shouts, in far too loud of a voice.

I grimace and put my pillow over my head.

Ataksak walks over and yanks it off almost instantly, throwing it to the floor. "Time to get ready, lady sunshine, training starts in ninety minutes, and we still need to get you down to the dining hall and through the breakfast line. So buckle up kiddo, it's going to be a rough first day."

Ataksak rummages through drawers and wardrobes, pulling out some clothes that she says are a "training uniform." She then states she will be back in twenty minutes, and I had better be wearing it and ready to go.

She speeds out the door, as quickly as she came, the door closing behind her. It's day two, and I've already noticed that she never stops moving.

I gently remove myself from this heavenly bed, and head for the bathroom.

Twenty minutes slip by quickly. I try to braid my hair like Ataksak's from yesterday, but it ends up looking nothing like hers. Still, it does the job and keeps the hair out of my face.

I've dressed in the training clothes Ataksak left out, and by the time she returns, I am as ready as I'll ever be for whatever is happening today.

Ataksak looks me up and down. "You look like you belong in Night."

I look down at myself, and then shrug. "I'm making the best of things."

Ataksak smiles. "I like you, kid. You don't ask a lot of questions, and you seem to fit right in. You can call me Atta now."

I smirk. "Gee, thanks."

Atta laughs loudly, and starts heading for the door. "Come on, Ellie, we don't wanna be late!"

Wonderful, she seems to have decided I needed a nickname, too.

Breakfast is uneventful. There are no owl-men to be seen, and Atta drops me off and waits outside just like she did for dinner last night.

I don't see Jaysen or Brock anywhere, so I eat quickly and in peace. As I start to clean up my plate, Jaysen and Brock enter the hall.

"Hey, you," Jaysen says, flashing that irresistible puppy dog smile. "Sleep okay? Or were you too excited to see me this morning? Already done with breakfast?"

I laugh. "I slept great, and I am done already! Sorry, I thought maybe you guys already came through. I tried to eat fast to catch up with you."

His face clouds with concern. "You slept . . . great?"

"Uhm, yes? Was I not supposed to?" I ask nervously.

"I mean, I could barely sleep with all my nerves, but I'm glad you got some rest! I'm sure we will need it for today!" Jaysen shrugs.

Brock looks around, and whispers, "Someone said they are going to make us kill each other during our training, that's why people don't come back . . ."

Jaysen smacks Brock's arm. "Don't say that, man! Let's stay positive."

I shrug, unsure of what to say. I'm pretty sure today's going to be tough no matter what, but I don't think they'll make us kill each other—at least, I really hope they don't. Honestly, I'm not sure I have it in me.

I put on a brave face, and smile at the boys. "I'm going to head off to my Night Realm Chaperone, Atta. She seems like a stickler who doesn't like to be late."

"Well, hopefully we will see you on the other side again, Elliora . . ." Jaysen winks at me, takes my hand in his, and gives it a gentle squeeze before letting go and heading toward the food. I gather my things and make my way to the door of the dining hall.

Atta smiles when I walk out and yells, "Just in time!"

I head her way and we make our way down the hall and to the elevator.

We leave the lobby and take a short walk around the building before arriving at the training center. Though it's technically "on-property," it's separate enough that you have to step outside to get there. The path is bordered by neatly trimmed hedges, and the cool air feels sharper once we're outdoors. The training center's sturdy doors stand just ahead, a clear reminder that this is where the real challenges begin.

From the outside, the training center resembles a miniature colosseum, its rounded walls rising with elegance. Massive stone pillars flank the entrance, each carved with intricate engravings—dragons coiling fiercely, owls perched in silent watch, phoenixes rising in flames, lions roaring with strength, stars scattered like distant sparks, and more. I don't have time to study the details now, but I'm already certain I'll come back later to take it all in when I have the time. We had nothing quite like this in Swaylin.

We step through another set of arched glass double doors—and what do you know? The training center boasts a massive glass ceiling, too. Honestly, it takes my breath away in a whole new way. The glass arches overhead in a graceful curve that seems almost impossible, bending light and space itself. Inside, the building opens into one vast, airy space. Benches line the perimeter, and the entire floor is padded, covered in shades of blue that fade from a soft, pale hue in the center to deep, rich navy at the edges. About sixty people are already gathered here. Some stand quietly in the center, others sit along the benches, their murmurs filling the room with low, expectant energy.

The stars above glow a soft, light purple, shining through the glass ceiling. The walls are breathtaking—each surface covered by a mural that wraps around the entire room in a seamless 360-degree masterpiece. I'm lost in the swirling colors and intricate scenes when Atta's voice suddenly breaks through my thoughts, pulling me back to the moment. "Training today is five hours, there is a lunch break at three. I'll be around here and there. Try to keep your thoughts to yourself today, and stay out of trouble." She reaches out, clasps my shoulder, smiles, and walks off.

Suddenly, a sharp, piercing owl cry cuts through the air—then another follows, echoing through the vast space. Two owls glide gracefully through the colosseum doors, wings beating silently against the stillness. One of them I recognize instantly, its feathers shimmering in the soft light. They soar up to the sturdy beams above and settle there, their keen eyes scanning the crowd below with an unsettling calm. Then, a deep, thunderous roar shakes the room as a lion strides confidently through the doors, its powerful presence commanding every gaze.

The Swaylin summoned start screaming and running away, making their way to the edges of the room. For a reason I can't explain, I can sense that this lion is also a human. I'm the only one not terrified and running. The lion makes its way directly toward me. He creeps closer and closer until he is only about an arm's length away, and then lets out a mighty roar. I can feel his hot breath on my face, but I don't cower. I stand tall and don't say a word. The lion makes eye contact with me, and huffs. An owl cry pierces the room again, and the lion walks away. I turn to track the lion, when right before my eyes, he shifts.

A strong man appears where the lion just was, and I'm not shocked. It seems my Swaylin peers are completely horrified, though. There are gasps, shouts, and one girl actually faints.

This man is tall. He has very long blond hair that is untamed, almost like a lion's. He is dressed in a gray shirt and dark blue pants. He looks like a leader.

The rest of the Swaylin summoned make their way into the Coliseum and everyone starts explaining to them what they missed. Jaysen and Brock make their way over to me.

"Are you okay? I heard a lion shifter is here?" Jaysen says with a worried look on his face.

"I'm completely fine," I reassure him. I grab his hand and give it a squeeze. It seems to be how he comforts and reassures me, so I figure it's worth trying.

Both owls cry out sharply, and from the corner of my eye, I catch one swooping down in a sudden dive, coming so close it nearly grazes Jaysen's head. With swift precision, it snatches something off the ground nearby before fluttering back up to its perch.

It's the owl I recognize, and I can *feel* Pollux's presence in it.

There is something hanging from his talons. It looks like he plucked a snake off the ground and brought it up to the beams with him. He lets the snake go, and it wraps itself around the beam and stares down.

I'm starting to grow tired of all these new thoughts and feelings swirling inside me. Especially knowing, somehow, that the snake is more than just a creature; it's a person too.

The man who was once a lion yells in a booming voice, "WELCOME SUMMONED OF SWAYLIN! We will be with you shortly, please stand towards the center of the training facility as we wait for the great King Canis to join us."

There are hushed whispers: everyone is shocked to hear we will see the king again so soon. In Swaylin I don't think I've ever seen the king in person. Now, I'll see this new king twice in a twenty-four hour period.

The tension in the colosseum is thick enough to cut through. No one utters a word; a stunned silence blankets the vast space.

A low rumble shakes the ground outside, quickly followed by another. I whip my head toward the massive arched doorway just as a shadow looms into view.

Then, suddenly, there is a giant foot. A dragon's foot? It can't be real... can it?

The room seems to hold its breath at the view of the vast, terrible, and breathtaking dragon before us. Its massive form casts shadows across the room, and its scales gleam in the starlight. I can't move or breathe at the sight of the monster before me. Its eyes meet mine, burning coals of ancient power. It's beautiful, yet I'm terrified.

I feel small, smaller than I ever have before. Suddenly the foot before me turns into King Canis, King of the Night Realm, and apparently . . . a Dragon Shifter?

And in that instant, I wasn't sure if I had come face to face when an ancient creature—or met a god.

He strides into the Coliseum, radiating the same formidable power I felt the last time I was in his presence. Behind him, two owls glide silently, ascending to join their companions perched high on the wooden beams.

King Canis moves at a deliberately slow pace, locking eyes with as many of us as possible along the way. When his gaze finally meets mine, a sharp pain shoots through my head. I don't flinch or show it. I hold steady eye contact and keep my expression unreadable. A smirk curls on his lips, and then diverts his eyes to the next Swaylin summoner.

When he reaches the center of the room, he draws his sword—the one with the intricately carved dragon winding around the hilt—and gently taps the blade's tip against the floor. The cold steel clicks sharply in the silence. Slowly, a small circular section of the ground begins to shift, grinding upward with a low, ominous rumble, as if awakening from a long slumber.

King Canis puts his sword back in its scabbard, and bellows "WELCOME!" He smiles widely and continues, "The Night Realm welcomes you and hopes you've had a pleasant first day here. We hope you continue to see the beauty of the Night Realm, and all it can offer you. Should you need anything during your time at the palace, please just ask! We are more than happy to accommodate you all, as best as we possibly can!"

He pauses and spins around on his platform to see those behind him. "I'm sure you are all wondering why you are here. Well, there are a few reasons. First and foremost, we are looking for the one to fulfill the prophecy. Evil lurks beyond the mountains to the north, in the Shadow Realms." His lips curve downward slightly. "Our enemies shall be defeated by those from the Day Realm who have the dark fire magic coursing through their veins."

"The other reason you are here is to find my other half, the one who shall fulfill the other half of our prophecy, marry me, and save our realms." His lips curl into a slow, cruel smile, a dark gleam flickering in his eyes like a predator savoring the hunt.

"The realms will be safe at last! When we finally find the ones we are searching for. Our special seekers in the Day Realm have scouted for you all throughout the years. They select those who they believe could harness the dark fire magic within them to travel here and attempt to fulfill our prophecies. Over the next several weeks, we will place you all into intense training with assigned groups. If you have the dark fire magic within you, you will move on to bigger and better things. Protecting us all, including those you love back home. However, if you don't have the magic at the end of the next sixteen weeks, we will let you choose. The same choice as all those who have come before you previously: live out your days in the Night Realm however you choose, or travel home to Swaylin. The choice will be yours."

There is a long pause before one brave man from Swaylin raises his hand in the air. He's tall with gorgeous golden hair, blue eyes, and the signature sun-tanned Swaylin skin. The king nods to him, gesturing for him to speak.

"What if we harness the dark fire magic within us, but we don't want to help? What if we want to travel home in the end?" the brave man says.

The king smirks, tilting his head just enough to nod toward the owls perched above. His voice drops low, laced with a deadly promise.

"Oh, if you wield dark fire magic, you'll want to stay. Trust me."

Chapter Eight

After the king's final, ominous words, silence hangs heavy in the air. Then, without warning, two owls burst into flight, wings beating sharply against the stillness. The platform beneath the king slowly descends back into the floor with a grinding echo, and he begins his slow, commanding walk out of the Coliseum. Every step is a reminder of the power he wields.

The silence continues to stretch amongst all of us, as we wait for whatever comes next.

The room hums with nervous energy. Tension thickens the air, sharp and heavy, mixed with the unmistakable scent of sweat. I force my face into a mask of calm, determined not to let a single flicker of doubt betray what I'm really feeling.

I glance up at the owl, who I know to be Pollux. His head spins ever so slightly, locking his piercing gaze onto mine. A sudden chill races down my spine, prickling my skin like icy fire.

I can't shake the feeling that I've seen him before. In a dream, maybe, but that can't be right. His eyes are different, and we only just met.

I glance back at the brave Swaylin man who spoke up earlier. He still looks calm compared to all the others. I don't recognize him from Swaylin, but I believe he is the other Swaylin summoned from my floor, floor eleven. I've only seen two of us on the eleventh floor, and judging by the doors, I think there are only four rooms on our floor to begin with.

I look around again to find Jaysen and Brock towards the back. Jaysen gives me a small smile and a wave. Brock whispers something to Jaysen, and then Atta walks into the building.

"Helloooooooooooo!" she shouts as she heads towards the spot where the king was just moments ago. "Boy, you guys could use some energy! How about a few laps around the Coliseum?!"

There is silence in response.

"Oh sorry, hi, I'm Ataksak. I'm here to train you for our morning session. We will run through some very basic tasks and then break for lunch. After lunch, we will break off into groups, which you will remain in for the duration of your training trials." She smiles. "So let's run some laps!

Four laps around the Coliseum is one mile. Start running, and GOOOO!" She points to the arched double doors with two fingers.

People start to move, so I break into a brisk walk. I'll wait to run until I'm outside. I'm near the center, but some are still frozen in place, so I weave around them, slipping through the crowd and out the doors as quickly as I can.

The moment I'm through the double doors, I break into a run. Not to sound cocky, but a mile's nothing. I used to race around our farm constantly as a kid, and kept it up through my teens. The faster I ran, the sooner I could escape the sun and get back to reading inside.

I make my way around the Coliseum. It is an oval-shaped building, which makes running feel pretty simple, and doing four laps is monotonous, but easy.

As I close in on the end of my third lap, there are a few people who are finishing their mile, but there are also a lot of people still behind me. I get the sense I'm somewhere amongst the middle.

The mile goes by fast, and a member of the Night Realm writes down my pace as I finish.

I head back in the double doors. Ataksak is right where I left her. Those who have finished are standing around waiting. Ataksak smirks at me as I go back to where I was standing before.

After a few more minutes almost everyone is back in their places. A few are still running, but it seems whatever time Ataksak was waiting on is up as she announces the next task.

We run through the basics: one hundred push-ups, one hundred sit-ups, and one hundred pull-ups. My muscles are shaking at the end of the pull-ups. In every category I wasn't the fastest, but I also wasn't even close to the slowest either.

They announce that in a few minutes we will break for lunch.

I lie on the floor, staring up at the stars through the glass roof. There's a quiet peace in them—something I've never felt before. Despite everything I don't know, everything that's still ahead, I feel at home here. Strangely, this unfamiliar place brings me more comfort than home ever did.

I bring my arm up to grab my water canteen and notice a single freckle glowing on my left arm. I quickly cover it and look up to the rafters.

Pollux's owl eyes are slightly slanted, unblinking, and fixed directly on me. There's something too knowing in that gaze, something that makes the hairs on the back of my neck rise.

Just then, Jaysen walks up and asks, "Hey, are you okay? What's wrong with your arm? Do you need any help?"

He reaches down to grab my right hand, which is currently covering the glowing freckle. I pull my arm back towards me. "No, I think I just got a little paper cut or splinter or something. It should heal up quickly." I smile up at him.

Jaysen's smile fades. "Okay, but if you're injured, promise you'll take care of it? Okay?" I glance back to where Pollux still watches me. Jaysen follows my gaze, to the rafters where the owls are sitting. "The owl thing is creepy, right? What do you think it's all about?"

Just then, Pollux lets out a screech, and dives with the other owls towards Jaysen. They all fly past his head at an alarming speed.

Jaysen ducks and barely misses the claws of Pollux. All owls exit the Coliseum, just as Ataksak lets us know it's time to move out for lunch.

"Please head to the dining hall at this time." She smiles around the room at all of us.

Everyone starts moving. I wait a minute to let some of the crowd pass before heading out. I glance over and Jaysen is there smiling and waiting for me. "Walk with me?" he says, holding his hand out to grab mine.

I don't reach for it, though. I feel like he is drawing unwanted attention to me.

We drift quietly toward the back of the group, our footsteps soft against the path. I don't mind the silence between us, it suits me, but I can almost hear it gnawing at chatty Jaysen beside me.

"How are you feeling? Is your cut okay?" he asks, striding along next to me.

"What?" I respond. "Oh! Yeah, uh . . . " I glance at my arm. "It's fine. It's not even there now." I hold up my arm to show him.

"Oh, good." He lets out a heavy sigh.

I quicken my pace, eager to avoid any more small talk.

We slip into the building, where conversation becomes pointless as the noise swells around us, bouncing off the walls. Voices rise and fall, echoing through the halls lined with glass, tile, and polished crystal, each surface amplifying the chaos.

Jaysen and I make our way to our usual spot, where Brock waits with two girls I vaguely recognize from the Day Realm.

We sit down for a few minutes. I roll out my wrists and ankles; I'm already tired. My body has been stationary for a while now. I'm definitely not in shape enough for one hundred pull-ups, but I'm happy I accomplished them anyway.

After a few minutes, we realize we need to go get our own food today, buffet style. We walk up and get in line.

I'm standing in the back of the line, behind Jaysen, when another boy walks up behind me.

"Hey," he whispers.

I glance over my shoulder at him. It's the guy who resides on the eleventh floor with me. The only other one from the Day Realm I know who is staying that high.

"Oh, hey!" I whisper back.

"How's the Night Realm treating you?" he asks with a smile.

"Uh, it's going okay, I think." I pause. "What about you?"

"Same." He nods at me, gesturing that the line in front of me is moving. I take a few steps forward. He taps me on the shoulder. "I'm Arcturus. I'm curious, do you know why we are the only ones to reside up on the eleventh floor? Or why we seem to be pointed out in some way? I can't for the life of me think of a reason," he mumbles.

Jaysen turns around then after finishing his conversation with Brock and the girls in front of him.

"Oh hey, Arc, how's it going?" He smiles at Arcturus, and shakes his hand.

"Going great, Jay, how about you? Enjoying this new world yet?" He laughs a little, but it's a nervous laughter.

Obviously, none of us are dumb enough to speak ill of the Night Realm at this point in time.

"It's good, man. I've made a new friend," he says while smiling over at me. "I also got to get a workout in today, so I can't complain too much."

"Cool, well I see my friend over there, gotta go," Arcturus mumbles, while gesturing over to a table with a few guys at it.

He exits the line and moves over to the table he was pointing at, taking a seat there and starting a conversation with someone.

"Huh, that was odd," I whisper to Jaysen.

"What was?" Jaysen asks.

"He just . . . he didn't get food." I turn to look at Jaysen. He's still smiling at me, looking happy and carefree, even though we are still unsure what we are training for or where we will be tomorrow.

Jaysen shrugs. "Maybe he just wanted to chat with you, I know I would. He probably has food already at the table." Jaysen turns back around.

"Yeah . . . maybe," I mutter under my breath.

Chapter Nine

AFTER WE GET SOME food down, Ataksak shouts into the dining hall, "Next is a series of puzzles that will take place in the recreation room just next door, in the room to your left. Please exit the dining hall in an orderly fashion and make your way there now."

We navigate into the recreation room. Desks are scattered throughout, and a large platform looms at the front. Ataksak, Pollux, and a few vaguely familiar faces are already gathered there.

A low hum settles over the space as the chatter dies away, a sudden hush blanketing the room like a held breath.

Once everyone is inside, Ataksak bellows out again, "Don't be shy, find a desk! There are desks for everyone. At each desk, you will find a series of puzzles. You will do your best to complete as many puzzles as possible within the next hour." She pulls her stopwatch timer out and yells, "You may begin."

There is mass chaos as everyone hustles to find a seat. I remain calm; an extra minute won't make a difference to me. I'll find a seat after everyone else gets one.

Jaysen yells from a few feet away, "Elliora! Over here!" I glance over just in time to see a girl take the seat he saved for me. He starts shouting at her.

"It's fine, Jaysen! Just start your puzzles!" I walk to find a seat now. The hairs on the back of my neck stand, and a chill sweeps my back. I glance at Pollux because, for some reason, that's where my eyes immediately go. He glances my way at the same time there is a large boom from the entrance of the room.

Every head snaps in the direction of the noise, and in walks King Canis. He saunters towards Ataksak at the front of the room. The people around her move to make room, as someone brings a throne from the side of the room.

He takes his seat without a word. Everyone glances around, waiting for some kind of extra instruction, but nothing comes.

I quietly slide into an empty chair and turn my attention to the puzzles, wasting no time.

There are riddles that require a written answer, puzzle pieces to put together a visual puzzle, math puzzles, word puzzles, pattern puzzles, and really every kind of puzzle you can possibly think of.

I move through the puzzles at a decent pace; some of them are harder than others. When I reach the final puzzle, it is something I've never seen before. After glancing at it, I look around. I don't see anyone near me working on this puzzle yet . . . I stare at it for a long time.

It looks like a random picture of the stars, and I keep staring at it because it looks oddly familiar to me. It can't be familiar, though, I haven't even seen stars in person until two days ago. Unless . . .

I hold it up towards the ceiling, and turn the image slightly. I bring the paper back down and draw a line connecting some of the stars. When I draw a few lines together, it looks similar to a dog with a triangular-shaped head. Although, I'm not sure if that was the point of the puzzle. I set my pen down and look to the front where all of the leadership stands.

They are all looking right at me, as if they knew I just finished. King Canis stands and strides toward me. I glance at Pollux, who has his hands at his sides in fists. His face is stern, jaw clenched like he is experiencing physical pain.

My eyes shift back to King Canis, and he's suddenly just a foot away. He steps up beside my chair, far too close for comfort. Still, I don't flinch. I stay rooted, refusing to move a muscle.

He immediately reaches for the picture of the stars. He picks it up and looks at it.

"How did you know which stars to connect?" he says loudly.

Every head whips my direction.

Great, more unwanted attention.

"I'm not sure, I was just trying something. There weren't instructions for that one," I state.

"Hm, curious," he mumbles.

He glances at the front nodding to Ataksak. She comes marching over. "Yes, my King?" she asks, with a small bow.

"Please take Miss . . ." he glances at me, as if asking my name.

"Elliora" I tell him.

He smiles. "Please take Miss Elliora to her room for some rest, and make sure she is fed properly."

"Oh, I'm quite okay here . . . " I start to say.

The corners of his mouth curl into a faint, unsettling smile. "No, no... I insist," he says, his voice smooth but edged with something darker.

Ataksak reaches out to help me stand, but I don't take her hand. I rise on my own, chest lifted, and stride proudly out of the Recreation Room. I avoid making eye contact with anyone, though I can feel their gazes burning into me.

At the exit, I steal a quick glance at King Canis—still in the same spot, that same unsettling smile fixed on his face. Nearby, Pollux's hands are clenched into tight fists at his sides. A man standing beside him rests a steady hand on Pollux's shoulder, as if holding him back from stepping toward me.

I turn my head deliberately, chin high, and keep moving down the hall.

Chapter Ten

AFTER THE SCENE IN the recreation room, Ataksak takes me to my room.

"Well, you certainly just caused an epic tizzy." She laughs.

"What are you talking about? All I did was draw some lines?" I seethe. "I don't even know if they were right."

"Oh, they were right, and no one has ever gotten them right. Not anyone from the Day Realm, at least. Most people in Night Realm don't even know the proper lines . . ." her voice trails off, and she moves into my bathroom. I hear her start the bath.

She comes back out.

"Food will be sent up from the king. I recommend eating a decent amount if you don't want him storming up here," she states.

"Why in all the realms would he come up to my room? Surely the king of a whole damn realm has better things to do than to make sure some insignificant girl from the Day Realm has eaten?" I question.

"You are no longer insignificant. You were already on everyone's list to watch, and I'm afraid those little lines you drew just made you suspect number one." She looks at me with a tense gaze. A chill runs down my back.

"Suspect? What in the god's name for? I don't understand," I cry.

"For the prophecy. You are likely destined now to be Queen of the Night Realm." She says it so off-handedly, I swear I must've heard her wrong.

"QUEEN?" I shout.

"Shush, keep it down," Ataksak says.

"Like as in . . . a wife to . . . to . . . married to . . ." I point towards the door, my stomach bottoming out. I think I'm going to be sick.

The king is handsome, don't get me wrong, but he has something mean in him. Every time I've been in his presence, I see a darkness in him.

On top of that, I always imagined that *if* I ever married, it would be for love. I've spent so much of my life alone, I know I can be content on my own. So if I never find someone truly special, then so be it. I'd rather stay alone than settle.

"Yeah, yeah, well now I gotta take care of you even more. Ugh." She rolls her eyes, as if this is all perfectly normal, like this conversation isn't unraveling the very fabric of my life.

"I mean, I had this strange feeling you would end up being a problem for me. I felt something powerful resting inside you, but I really hoped I was wrong. It would've been way easier for me." She laughs.

She prances back into the bathroom.

"Alright. Bath is ready, food should be here soon. I'm going to run off to grab a few things and have a few conversations. I'll be back in a bit." She turns and makes her way out the door.

I just stand there, frozen, either in a state of panic or shock. I'm not entirely sure. My brain can't process fast enough to tell the difference.

Standing in the middle of the room, I just stare at the door she just walked out of, as if it might open again and undo everything. Minutes pass by before I finally let my clothes fall in a heap at my feet, and drift toward the bathtub.

I won't pretend I wasn't looking forward to another shower, those are honestly still a novelty to me. But when I walk into the bathroom, and spot the steam curling from the tub with the soft purple hue of the scented water, something in me relaxes. I'm ready to sink into it, and completely disappear for a while.

I step in and sink down low into the tub. I play with the bubbles, blowing in the water with my mouth, while staring at my toes peeking out of the other end.

There is a sharp knock on the door of my room, followed by the sound of the door opening. I pause when I realize that I left the bathroom door wide open.

Ataksak will probably see me naked at some point anyway, so I just sit there alone with my thoughts. When I finally glance over to the bathroom door, I see Pollux standing in the doorway holding a tray of food.

He is gripping the tray so hard that I'm afraid it might break in half.

"I'm sorry," he rasps. "I'll just leave this in the sitting area." He moves quickly away from the door. I hear loud noises and then an obnoxious groan.

"You okay?" I shout.

Footsteps move back toward the bathroom doorway.

"Do you need anything else, Miss Elliora?" he grunts.

"So formal now." I sigh. "Want to wash my back for me? I have the hardest time reaching back there," I joke.

Pollux keeps his face masked with anger.

"It was a joke. See ya later owl-man." I salute him, almost accidentally displaying a breast to him. "Whoops," I say, as he storms out of the room.

The door to my room slams shut abruptly behind him.

I sink down into the water.

I'm alone.

Not just for this moment, and maybe not even just for today.

I'm just really *alone*.

I think about the isolation in my life. I truly have no one, and I mean, I never have, but in a new place with new people . . . it's even harder. I thought this would be a fresh start for me, but it's quickly turning into misery again.

For a moment, I consider just ending it all. I could just drown myself here and now, save myself from perhaps living a completely miserable life.

Who would even miss me? No one. I don't even think Jaysen would lose sleep if I just ended this miserable life here and now.

Although, I've already survived a lot of misery back home. I'm feeling more at home and at peace since entering the Night Realm than ever before. I might as well at least try this new life out. See what I can make of it. I can always drown myself later to put an end to it all.

If I end up being queen, though... I just, I don't think that is a good fit for me. I've never even considered a life of nobility. I've always been nobody. Even back in Swaylin, I couldn't seem to make a friend. How could I possibly inspire a realm? That's what nobility is supposed to do right? Inspire their people? Bring about change, and justice. I can't even change my own life, how could I possibly change a realm if I needed to?

I can feel my heart pounding in my chest at each thought, each beat loud and insistent. Panic floods my veins, sharp and unrelenting. My head throbs, and I press my fingers to my temples, trying to apply pressure to take the ache away. The warmth of the bath, which was comforting a few minutes ago, now feels suffocating. I decide it's time to get out; it's not helping anymore.

I get out and grab a towel and dry off and wrap it around my body. I make my way into the other room to the tray of food Pollux brought up.

Everything looks delicious: the plate is full of an array of meats, fresh fruits, and colorful vegetables. There's even a sweet dessert on the plate, something delicate and tempting. I want to eat it all, I really do. But my stomach is twisted tight in knots with nerves. After a few failed attempts, I set the food down and quietly retreat to my new favorite place, the bed.

I lay flat on my back and stare up at the stars through the glass ceiling. I'm still wearing only a towel. I lay there gazing up for so long, I slowly start to doze off before being woken up abruptly by the return of Ataksak.

"I thought I told you to eat a decent amount!" she shouts from the sitting area.

"I can't stomach it," I whine.

"Ugh! You're going to be a pain in my ass now, aren't you?" She makes her way in.

I pick my head up off the bed to glance at her.

"Dear lord. You really are going to be a pain. Are you laying in your towel still? Jeez." She sighs. "Well, get up. Get some clothes on, in case someone needs to come see you in a bit. I'm heading to a meeting with the king and the rest of the King's Guard. I imagine it'll be a meeting to tell me your suspect number one, but I'll act surprised." She winks at me, while rummaging through the drawers of the dresser.

She throws a pair of pants and a shirt onto the bed next to me.

"Why tell me all of this? Shouldn't it still be a secret or something?" I mutter under my breath.

"Eh, probably. However, I've made it this far in my life by being honest and blunt. Ain't no use in changing myself now. Plus, I like you. You've got spunk, kid." She smiles widely.

I laugh. "I'm like, what, five years younger than you?"

"Yeah, yeah, something like that." She winks at me before lazily walking towards the door.

"Do me a favor and just don't get into any trouble until I'm back. You're currently making me look pretty damn good and I'd like to keep it that way." She tilts her head in a nod, before heading out the door.

I lay there for a few more minutes, staring up at the stars to steady my racing heart. After a deep breath, I push myself up from the bed and change into the clothes Ataksak left for me. Naturally, they fit perfectly.

After getting dressed, I stand there for a moment, glancing around the room. It's . . . quiet. Too quiet, maybe. There's honestly nothing in here to do, not unless I want to stare at the walls. I shift my weight from one foot to the other, arms loosely crossed.

I *could* go wander the halls, right? I mean... she *did* say our free time was ours, to do what we want. I think? Or at least, that's how I remember Atta saying it.

But still, is that *really* what she meant? I can just roam around? Would that be weird? Maybe. Probably not.

I sigh and glance at the door, then back at the room. Yeah . . . maybe I'll just take a walk. See where it leads, and help clear my head. It's just a little stroll, and I can't stay here any longer.

I slowly make my way to the door and ease it open, just enough to peek out into the hallway. It's empty, eerily so. There is no sign of any movement on my floor.

Taking a deep breath, I slip out and head toward the elevators. My footsteps are light, careful, the kind of steps you take when you're not entirely sure you're supposed to be walking around. I press the call button, and just as the soft chime dings in response, I hear footsteps echo from around the corner.

I freeze.

From the far end of the hall, a large figure emerges; it's one of the King's Guard members. He moves with purpose, sword glistening faintly under the starlight as he disappears into a nearby door. Recognition flickers somewhere within me. I think I saw him earlier today. He was stationed at the front during the puzzle trials, and with the sharpness in his gaze... I'd guess he's an owl-man too.

Before I can stop myself, my feet are already moving.

In seconds, I find myself standing just outside the door he entered. My heart is beating in a quick rhythm. Muffled voices rise from inside. They are loud, intense, but just too jumbled to make out clearly.

Something important is happening in there.

I'm not sure if I should stay and listen, or turn back before I get caught.

I take one step closer to the door and hold my breath, trying to see if I can hear anything. It's no use though, all I can hear are mumbles. I would give absolutely anything right now to be a fly on the wall for the king's conversation...

My skin itches like it doesn't fit right. Something inside me stirs. I can't just stand here. I need to do something.

My spine arches as a change begins, sudden and unstoppable. My muscles clench involuntarily, like they have a mind of their own. Heat flares across my chest, like something inside me is waking up. My arms stretch wide, fingers fusing into a sweeping curve of wings. While my knees buckle, reform, hollow, and lean.

A pain roars across my body.

Suddenly, I'm in the room. Panic grips me.

How did I get here? How did I get in the room?

Instinctively, I reach for my chest, but I can't. My breathing is shallow as my voice fails. I'm... I'm a fly, a literal fly on the wall.

My heart pounds in my tiny body as I struggle to comprehend what's happening to me. I try to breathe, I try to steady myself, but each exhale comes out as a soft, vibrating buzz.

I cling to the wall, impossibly small. I'm invisible to everyone. I'm a powerless observer.

I try to focus. This is what I wished for mere seconds ago. I look around the room.

King Canis sits in an impossibly large chair, while everyone else stands around in a circle surrounding him. Ataksak, Pollux, and other members of the King's Guard are arguing loudly.

"That's enough!" the king bellows, and the room turns absolutely silent.

"I want eyes on the girl every second of the day, until we know the truth. But for now we assume she is the one from the prophecy, we assume she is the one to be my wife," he states. The way he says it, so calm and certain, like my opinion doesn't even matter, makes my blood boil.

My eyes shift to Pollux: he's standing in the same rigid pose he always does. His jaw clenched, fists tight, shoulders wound up like coiled springs. Honestly, the guy looks like he could use a massage, no one can hold that much tension all day without hurting.

I glance at Ataksak, who is smiling off to the side. She is the picture of calm, the polar opposite of her dear friend Pollux.

Suddenly, one of the men snaps his head to the door, and then up in my direction. I'm pretty sure it's the lion from the Coliseum earlier today.

"What is it?" the king asks him, leaning forward in his chair.

"I . . . I feel . . . It feels like she's in here," he mumbles.

Everyone in the room begins to whisper amongst themselves, looking around.

The king stands up and walks over the man. "Hmm, well go on. Keep using your powers then. Where is she? Has she manifested her magic? Does she wield the power of invisibility?" He sighs. "It would be a tragic waste if she did, as it would rule her out as the one from the prophecy."

The man continues looking around the room, my heart starts pounding heavily again.

Pollux shifts his weight on his feet, looking around uncomfortably.

I close my beady insect eyes, and breathe. How did I end up here? I wished I was a fly on the wall... Maybe I can just un-wish it or wish for something else.

Taking deep breaths, I repeat it over and over. I wish to be out of here, free from this situation. *I wish to be out of here. I wish to be out of here.*

Another pain strikes my chest, another tingling sensation runs over my body. I am eager to be out of this room and out of this insect body that is not my own. I close my eyes tightly, feeling my body contort and move in ways I never imagined, and suddenly hear a collection of gasps.

When I open my eyes, I'm standing in the center of the circle. The king smirks at me. "Well hello there . . . how utterly disappointing, we were hoping you would be something more . . . magnificent . . ." He looks me up and down, and it sends nausea through my stomach. The way his eyes glisten as he stares.

I glance down at my feet, but they aren't feet. A pair of massive gray furry paws greet me. I look back at Pollux, who is now behind me, glaring.

My eyes move to Ataksak, who smirks, like she just fucking knew all along.

"But sir..." the man who said earlier he thought I was here speaks. "How did she get in here?" he whispers.

My head whips back to the king, whose eyebrows draw together in confusion. "I . . . huh, how *did* she get here like this?" He looks me up and down again.

"I wonder . . ." he murmurs.

"Come, everyone . . . It seems we need to take a little field trip with my new pet." He smirks, winks, and my stomach churns. He stands abruptly, and begins to make his way out of the room.

Ataksak comes up and pats me on the head. "Good girl," she says with a laugh. A snarl rips from my throat, followed by an intense growl that's enough to startle even myself.

"Awww, that was so cute, follow me babe," she says, and she turns and walks toward the door. I prowl behind her, trying to move in my new body without making a complete fool of myself. I take slow, concentrated steps toward her. When I get close to the door, my head snaps toward footsteps from behind me.

Pollux stands there, his eyes glowing, sharp and still like an owl's in the night. We don't move, we are just two animals, sizing each other up in the silence before something breaks.

I snarl, before turning back to Ataksak and following her out the door.

We make our way down the hall to the elevator. I stand outside of it, staring. I'm afraid my large frame will take up too much room, but Ataksak tells everyone around us, "Just Elliora and I in this one . . . You guys grab the next."

The elevator doors open, and I make my way inside. Ataksak presses the button for the lobby, and just before the doors shut, Pollux grabs the door and pushes his way in.

"Maybe you didn't hear me, *buddy*," she snaps. "But I said her and I only in this one," she growls.

"Oh I heard you Atta, I just don't give a shit," he bites back.

I growl loudly at both of them. Their heads whip to me, distracted, as the elevator doors close. I sit down, unsure of my body and legs.

Pollux and Ataksak stare at me. Pollux whispers to Atta, as though I'm not even there, "Did you know?"

"I had an idea, but I'm worried there is more to this," she says, gesturing to me. "I thought she was the one from the prophecy . . . I bet on it in fact." She smirks.

Pollux grunts, "A heads up would've been nice Atta. This is bad." He glares at her.

"It's fine. Unless there is more . . ." She looks at me, and then back to Pollux. "Besides, what do *you* care? So what if she is the one from the prophecy . . . why is *she* different?" She raises her eyebrows at him in question.

"I..." he starts, but the elevator doors ding open, and I prowl out. I need to get away from them. I have this strange urge to bolt out the front doors.

"Wait!" Ataksak calls after me, but it's too late. I'm too fast. I fly out the front doors and straight into King Canis.

"Oh hello, my dear," he purrs. It makes my stomach sick.

Pollux and Ataksak come running out the front doors, just as King Canis goes up in a cloud of purple smoke. I cough and stumble back a step.

Before me towers a massive dragon, its scales a shimmering blend of violet and shadow. It unleashes a thunderous roar that rattles the stones beneath my feet. All around, doors creak open and curious faces begin to emerge from windows.

The people of Canopus cheer when they see him. Some even get down on their knees and start worshipping him in prayer.

Even in his dragon form, his face stirs the same anger in me. Rage coils in my gut, and fire surges through my veins like molten steel.

The same vile smirk is somehow still there, etched in the lift of his maw, in the wisp of smoke that escapes his nostrils. I know that look. He knows exactly what he's doing: he's playing with me, relishing every second.

He bends over, his face horribly close to Ataksak and Pollux. He starts to move like he is going to attack them.

My body revolts. It's like something inside me snaps. The moment I see them threatened, every other thought burns away. There's no room for reason, no time for hesitation. My chest tightens, heart pounding like war drums, and suddenly the now-familiar pain hits my chest. The tingling sensation sweeps my body.

There is a surge of fire flooding my veins, and I *have* to step in. The world narrows to a single truth: they are mine to protect, and whoever dares harm them will face me.

King Canis stands, moving away from them, as a silver mist erupts out around me. My body shifts, as heat dances down my spine. My skin ripples into iridescent scales, shimmering like silver liquid. Bones crack, stretching and moving, until I'm eye level with the King. Wings tear from my back with a loud snap.

I look down at Pollux and Ataksak. They are safe on the ground, staring at me wide-eyed. A look of shock, or maybe panic, etched across their faces.

My head snaps back toward King Canis, the big smiling dragon before me.

I glance at the street of Canopus, where everyone stands staring up at us. Most of them are on their knees in praise.

I let out a thunderous roar that shakes the world. I don't know why or how it came out of me.

Everyone in the streets covers their ears, and a single tear escapes my eye, before I black out.

Chapter Eleven

I WAKE UP DRENCHED in sweat. My body is roaring for water. Ataksak and Pollux are at the side of my bed, ready. Ataksak pours water over my skin as it sizzles. I look down and scream at the steam rising from it. Pollux pours some water in my mouth. I try to swallow but it burns my throat in a searing pain, and I can't seem to swallow.

Pollux whispers next to me, "Hey. Look at me." I turn my head and lock eyes with him. "You are going to be okay, you've got this." He slowly strokes my hair as he says it. A tear slides down my cheek. I can't seem to process my thoughts.

I'm trying to remember what happened, but it's like trying to remember details of a dream after already waking up. It's hazy, but the memories are slowly coming back in pieces.

A panic seizes my chest as I start to remember, I shifted. I shifted twice, no *shit*, three times.

Was that all a dream? It couldn't be real.

Pollux must see the panic on my face. I try to talk, but nothing comes out. I start coughing, and puffs of smoke come out. My chest tightens, and I can't breathe.

"Hey!" Pollux shouts, grabbing my shoulder. "You need to relax, you're panicking, and I get it, but you need to calm yourself down. This room has a spell on it to prevent you from shifting again for the next twenty-four hours. You're getting worked up . . . and your body wants to react, you need to try and take some deep breaths or you're going to pass out again."

I stare into his eyes, and focus on my breathing. Every breath feels weighted; it feels like a struggle just to breathe. Pollux continues to stroke my hair, calming me with his presence alone.

I glance back over to Ataksak, who looks sympathetic. Her eyes are glossy, as she still holds the cup of water. I look down at my skin, which is starting to feel normal again. I close my eyes and think about things that have made me happy recently.

I have friends, or at least acquaintances, who I consider friends. Which is more than I've ever had before. I get to sleep under the stars every night now, and that provides peace I've never known. I got to experience life on a ship, and realize how much I loved it. I don't have to worry about plants dying, or the sun burning my skin for the distant future.

I keep circling through these positive things in my mind, until breathing doesn't feel as hard. It no longer feels like each breath is a chore.

I open my eyes, and Ataksak and Pollux are looking at each other. It honestly looks like they are having a whole conversation, but I can't hear a word.

Ataksak glances back towards me. She stands up, squeezes my shoulder, and then turns and leaves the room.

My eyes don't move from the door she just left out of. I'm trying to calm my racing heart, trying to make sense of everything that just happened. Everything that just changed.

I shifted. I shifted three times.

I... I didn't know magic existed. Now here I am in the Night Realm, and I myself have magic. As I process what this means a few more tears trickle down my face.

Will I ever see Grandpa again now? I didn't have high hopes when I left Swaylin . . . He's old, and I figured if I did return, I would be deemed 'insane' like the rest of them.

But now . . . now I don't think I'm ever going back.

I look back at Pollux. His infuriatingly handsome face is etched with sorrow or maybe disappointment, it's hard to tell. He lifts his arm, and gently wipes the tears from my face.

"Are you okay?" he whispers.

"Yeah," I whisper back, because I have to be strong, but I can't help thinking about how I almost tried to kill myself earlier, and now I don't know what happens next. So maybe I should have ended it when I had the chance.

I wake from a nap a few hours later. My breath is hot, as I roll over onto my back to look up at the stars. The past few hours, I've dozed in and out of sleep while Pollux and Ataksak took turns watching over me.

I lay there now, trying to guess what time it might be. I must have missed dinner, my stomach rumbles with the thought of food.

I get up, and my legs shake underneath me. I hold on to the dresser as I make my way to the door. I don't see Pollux or Ataksak anywhere right now.

I gently and quietly open the door, and look out into the hall. I start making my way to the elevator, when a hand grabs me.

"Ah!" I shout. Turning to see Ataksak standing there, a stern look on her face.

"What in all the realms are you doing?!" she seethes.

"I—I'm hungry," I growl.

She takes a step back, letting go of my arm gently.

"Fine, I'll get you food. Please return to your room," she mumbles.

"Am I a prisoner now? Can I not get my own food?" I hiss.

"You are not a prisoner, you are betrothed to the King of Canopus, and destined to fulfill a decades-long prophecy. Therefore, you can't be seen out in... that." She gestures to my clothes.

I gasp, looking down at my clothes and processing the words that she just spoke. "So it's official then? I'm betrothed to the king? I don't remember receiving a proposal?" The words come out harsh, my anger misplaced towards Ataksak.

Ataksak sighs. "You confirmed what we all thought the second you shifted to a dragon. Although, the fact that you can shift into multiple beings is . . . new for all of us. Even the king himself cannot do that, which has everyone wondering..." her voice trails off as she glances around the hall.

"Please return to your room, Elliora. I will bring you food," she whispers.

I look toward the elevators, and then turn back toward my room, and make my way back inside.

Once inside, I faceplant down into the soft mattress. I've loved being in the Night Realm, but I have a feeling I won't anymore. It no longer feels safe, and I no longer feel the peace I felt this morning, or yesterday morning? I don't know anymore. Everything is a blur now. Instead, I feel like a prisoner once again, and I'm not looking forward to what tomorrow and the future will bring.

There is a knock at the door, and I groan. I roll over and push myself off the mattress. My muscles and bones ache with every movement. I'm not sure if it's from the training that happened earlier, or the shifting my body just accomplished.

I can't believe the training was less than a day ago; it honestly feels like a different lifetime.

I take a deep breath before swinging open the door. Jaysen stands there disheveled. He's breathing heavily, and pacing in my doorway.

"Oh, thank the gods." He strolls into my room without asking. I grit my teeth, because I just want to eat and rest. The last thing I want is to host happy-go-lucky Jaysen.

"Holy shit this room is freaking nice!" Jaysen glances around the room.

He turns around to face me, and looks me up and down before reaching forward and grabbing my hands in his. "Are you okay? I've been so damn worried about you... They wouldn't let me talk to you, and there have been rumors..." He brings his voice down low and whispers, "that you are now betrothed to the King of Canopus, King Canis."

I roll my eyes. "I mean, he hasn't asked, but I've heard the same thing." The door swings open, and in walks Pollux and Ataksak.

Ataksak shakes her head in frustration while holding a tray of food, as Pollux glares at Jaysen. His jaw is tense, as he strides towards us with ominous steps.

He reaches Jaysen and grabs him by the shirt. "Get out. Now," Pollux seethes.

Jaysen looks at me, eyes wide with horror.

I'm so tired, I have no idea what's going on anymore. I try to give him a sorrowful glance, implying he should just leave.

Jaysen looks back at Pollux, who is still gripping his shirt with clenched fists. "Fine, but I'm her only friend here from Day Realm... I'm only here because I care!"

"Thanks, Jaysen, I'll see you tomorrow..." I glance at Pollux and Ataksak. "Hopefully." I shrug.

Pollux finally lets go of Jaysen, and he all but runs out of the room.

"He shouldn't have been in here," Pollux seethes. "I pray the king finds out and punishes him."

Ataksak snorts. "Okay ya big ol' meanie." She finally sets down the tray she's been holding. "Here is some food for you, my future queen. I recommend not opening the door for anyone else today. Eat, sleep, and bathe. Tomorrow will likely be an eventful day, and you need to return to full health by then." She glances at Pollux. "I'm leaving now, I suggest you leave too." She raises her brow at him, before turning and leaving the room.

Pollux stares at me for a long minute before finally speaking. "Are you okay? Are you feeling any better than earlier?"

"I'm okay, I just want to eat and rest more. I'll be fine..." I mutter.

"Okay, this is exactly what I didn't want to happen, El." He sighs. "I knew there was something special about you, and I didn't want to be right, I didn't want you to end up...his." He grimaces slightly.

My breath catches. "Oh," I manage, my voice barely above a whisper.

Heat blooms in my cheeks, sudden and betraying. I look down, pretending to adjust the hem of my shirt. My heart flutters with the erratic rhythm, like a bird taking off too fast.

I glance back up at him, and our eyes met again. He smiles, just a little. Or maybe I'm imagining it, but it's just enough. My heart does a happy little stumble again.

"I'll let you rest. Get some sleep, El," he mumbles, before exiting the room.

Chapter Twelve

I WAKE THE NEXT morning to Ataksak banging on my door before swinging it open and screaming, "Rise and shine, my little dragon lady and future queen!"

I groan.

My head is pounding as I sit up and rub my eyes. When I open them, Ataksak is staring at me. "I can't believe you're still in bed, it's beautiful today," she sings.

I throw myself back on to the pillow and look up at the ceiling. The stars glow a greenish hue today. Goosebumps pebble across my skin as I stare at them. Ataksak comes over and sits next to me on the bed.

"Listen, dragon girl, I've grown semi-fond of you, and I've now been tasked with being your servant basically all day, every day. Therefore, I'd like to be friends, and give you some advice?" She lets out a little laugh.

I meet her gaze and wish I felt something different, something better. I wish I could be her friend, but after the past twenty-four hours, I don't even know what's real anymore. I've never had a friend before, so how could I possibly be a good one now?

She sighs, almost as if she can see the resignation in my eyes. "Here's my advice, kid. Keep your head down, do what you're told, and trust no one. The time for you to shine will come, I know it will. Whatever you want, you will be able to have it. But only if you're patient and play the game."

I huff. "Atta, I'm a nobody from Swaylin who truly considered drowning myself in a bath yesterday. I have no friends, so trust isn't something I could do even if I wanted. Apparently, I'm going to be queen now of some godforsaken realm that makes people go insane. What in all the gods do you think I'm going to do? Start a riot? I don't fucking know anyone here, Atta," I yell.

I'm getting fired up. I'm sick of the people who seem to 'care'. No one, and I mean no one, gives a shit about me. Why the hell should I even be here?

"Aye!" Atta shouts, "There is some personality, I've been waiting for you to show some kind of emotion." She smiles.

"Come on, kid, let's get you some dinner." She stands up off the bed and starts rummaging through my drawers.

"Dinner?!" I shriek.

"Yep. You slept through breakfast and lunch, you little lazy wolf-dragon lady. Now let's head out, you've got some nighttime training this evening!" She walks over and disappears into the bathroom. I hear the water start running.

My body feels like a ton of bricks; it's stiff and hard to move, but I push myself out of bed. My eyes are heavy.

I move slowly, my body aches, but I make it to the bathroom to see a bath drawn and swirling with a blue soap.

"This soap will help with the pain. Sit and soak for at least five minutes. I'll be back in ten to take you down to dinner. And Ellie? Don't even think about trying to off yourself again. All eyes in the entire Night Realm are on you now. You owe it to yourself to give them a good show." Atta nods her head, and then turns to head out the door.

I sink into the tub and hum my favorite song from back home, because I know it's exactly five minutes long. I used to sing it to myself while farming to keep track of time.

When I finish humming my tune, I rise up out of the tub, and my body does feel slightly better. I dry off, and get dressed. I sit in one of the plush chairs for a minute while waiting for Atta to return.

When she finally does return, she smiles at the sight of me. "See? Night Realm looks good on ya, kid."

"Thanks," I mumble.

"Alright! Let's get this over with. Off to dinner, and then you're training with Pollux." She turns.

"Wait! Why Pollux?" I groan.

She turns and grins. "Because you need to learn how to shift properly."

"And he is the best one to do it?" I ask.

"He's the best one to do it." She smiles.

We enter the dining hall, and my eyes immediately find Pollux at the front of the room. He stands and watches over everyone as usual. I scan the room and eventually see Jaysen and Brock. I wave, and start making my way to them. They are sitting with two girls I vaguely recognize from Day Realm.

I reach them just as Atta hands me a platter of food, "From the King himself." She nods, and then walks away.

I groan.

"So, is it true?" Jaysen whispers.

"I don't know? What part?" I reply.

"You're betrothed to the king?" Brock whispers. "That you're the one they've been looking for?"

"Hm, I don't actually know. The king hasn't said anything to me, but it seems to be rumored that I am engaged . . . which is crazy, since I was never asked, and I definitely never said yes. I also don't know if I'm the one they were looking for. Wasn't there technically two they were looking for?" I take large mouthfuls of food into my mouth, in hopes they will change the subject.

It doesn't work.

Jaysen tries to reach for my hand, but I pick up my bread to keep him from grabbing it. The bread is still warm, and delicious. I will never get over how much better the food is in Night Realm.

Brock looks confused. "You must have some kind of idea as to why they think you're special?"

Jaysen glances at Brock. "Elliora is doing the best she can. Don't question her like that."

Brock looks annoyed with him. "Whatever." He gets up and leaves the table.

I continue to eat, and Jaysen starts talking to the other two girls about their training this morning.

I overhear one of them say, "I don't know why we are continuing, they clearly found *her*" before they get up and leave as well.

Jaysen sighs, and then turns to me. "Elliora, how are you? Are you okay?"

"I'm okay for now, Jaysen. I appreciate your friendship, but don't feel like you need to keep checking on me." I smile at him to try and drive the point home. It's clear his alliance with me is frustrating those around him.

"I promised your mom I'd keep an eye on you, and take care of you." He strokes my hand with his.

Alarms blare in my head. My mother doesn't care about me one bit. Why in the realms would she ask Jaysen to take care of me? She doesn't care if I live or die?

"Uhm, what?" I ask.

Pollux walks up and grunts. "You almost done? It's time to train."

I glance at him, and then back at Jaysen, who looks defeated to be interrupted by Pollux yet again.

"Sure." I take a big drink of water. "Thanks for being a good friend, Jaysen." I give his hand a squeeze before getting up and taking my tray of food to the trash station.

"He's not a good friend," Pollux mumbles next to me.

"Oh yeah, how would you know?" I glare at him.

"I . . ." Pollux sighs.

"Okay, well, he is all I have here, so why don't you continue to mind your own business?" I snap. I walk towards the doors in search of Atta.

I find her just outside the dining hall doors.

She looks at me, and then at Pollux. "Well don't you guys just look so chipper and ready to start your training." She laughs. "Alright, well, it looks like you already found your training buddy, Ellie. You guys have fun!" She salutes us, before heading off towards the stairs.

I look back at Pollux, and groan. "Where are we going?"

Chapter Thirteen

I'VE SPENT THE LAST three nights training with Pollux, and to be honest, I hate it. He's quiet and grumpy. I've yet to see him crack a smile. While that should put me at ease, since I'm used to people in my life being unhappy, it doesn't.

I have yet to hear anything else about my betrothal, or what in all the realms I am actually training for.

All I know is that I'm training how to shift in and out of wolf and dragon forms, because that is all Pollux knows about . . .

I don't know who to trust or how much to reveal, so I keep to myself the fact that I have also been a fly.

We've only been working on wolf, because Pollux said to start 'small'. Little does he know . . .

The room smells like sweat. I have yet to actually accomplish a shift during our three days of training. In fact, I've yet to shift since my dragon moment out in front of the palace with King Canis.

"Again," yells Pollux, arms crossed, his golden eyes glowing like a pair of torches. "You're holding back," he snaps.

"I'm not—" I croak. My teeth clench. I can feel my jaw pulsing, trying to change its shape. My voice is warping, turning from human to a low growl.

I fall on my knees, chest heaving, fingers clenching. The pain comes in pulses now. Waves of heat and pressure roll under my skin, my bones aching to reshape. But every time I get close to shifting, fear yanks me back.

"You *are*," Pollux steps forward, crouched low. His voice has lost its sharp edge. "You're afraid it's going to hurt. News flash—it *is* going to hurt. That's the point of training: to make it hurt *less*. The trick is wanting it more than you fear it."

I look up at him. His silhouette shimmers in the starlight. He is human still, but only barely. His muscles are tight, posture fluid, like his body can't decide which skin to wear.

I clench my fists tighter, grinding my teeth together.

Pollux crouches beside me, voice low and close. "Think of it like diving off a cliff. You can't shift halfway. You *jump*. You didn't think about it the first time you did it, you gave in, you did whatever it took. You just jumped."

I close my eyes. The wolf is pacing inside my ribs, pressing against my skin like it wants out. I let the heat come, let the bones start to grind and stretch.

My spine arches sharply, a scream tearing from my throat, then catching halfway into a snarl.

It feels like fire and glass and the moment before a lightning strike.

And then—

Silence.

I blink.

The world is brighter, louder, clearer. I can hear every heartbeat in the hallway outside as it thuds against my ears. I can *smell* Pollux's approval.

A low, triumphant growl escapes my throat.

Pollux grins. "I told you. You just had to jump."

That night, when I'm alone in my room, I decide to try shifting into a different form. I know I was a fly before, but I have this feeling I can be *more*.

I close my eyes and focus on what is deep within me.

I find an owl. My fingers tingle. The air is heavy with anticipation. A single candle flickers on the dresser with the stacks of books and old maps that I requested, and Atta brought me.

Outside, the stars glow bright, and I open up the window. I step back and stumble into the bed.

My shoulders hunch unnaturally, bones shifting beneath skin. Feathers prick through my back, first one, then dozens, bursting in a soft rustle. My fingers contort, shortening into curved talons as the candle sputters violently, then snuffs out.

The starlight becomes my only light.

My eyes widen, unblinking. My nose flattens, narrowing into a beak. The room around me seems to bend and stretch.

Seconds later, the transformation is complete.

I'm an *owl*—regal, silent, otherworldly—perching on the edge of the bed frame. My feathers are a patchwork of mottled gray and brown, starlight dancing off their texture. I blink once, slowly, and then fly out the open window.

I turn back, glancing at the room, my human life still hanging in the air like a perfume.

With a screech, I vanish into the night.

The candle flares back to life, though no one is left in the room to see it.

My wings cut through the air with a grace that feels both ancient and newly discovered. The cold bites, but I don't feel it. Every sense of mine is heightened. I hear a mouse rustle under a frost-covered plant five stories below. I smell the chimney smoke curling into the night air. I see in layers—heat, light, and shadow.

And yet, it's not just my senses. It's something else.

My world has changed.

Below me, the town glows in subtle colors I've never seen before. Buildings thrum with hidden energy. Roads, empty and silent, weave like veins through a living body. The forest beyond the town isn't just trees—it's moving, watching.

I bank sharply and rise high into the air, driven by instinct.

I'm above the clouds now.

I don't know what this place is, but something in my bones, in my feathers, knows. I belong here.

I drift in a slow, spiraling pattern. The wind carries me like a lullaby. My wings are growing tired now, feeling heavier with every beat.

The town appears below, familiar in shape but somehow smaller now. More fragile. I see the chimneys, rooftops, and finally my window.

I circle once, then dive, silent as a whisper.

I land softly on the windowsill. The candle still flickers, waiting. The room hasn't changed—but I have.

I hop down onto the wooden floor, claws clicking quietly. With a breath, my owl becomes human, slowly, like exhaling a dream. Bones shift, and my skin reclaims me. I'm back in my own form, shivering, kneeling on the cold floor.

Behind me, one single feather floats gently to the floor.

Chapter Fourteen

I'VE SPENT THE PAST few weeks in a heavy rotation of eating, sleeping, and training. Whenever I have a spare second alone, I train on my own.

I hone in on my shifting abilities. I've shifted into an owl, a fly, a python, a cat, a wolf, and a dragon. I only shift into a wolf in Pollux or Atta's presence. I don't trust anyone enough to share any more information than I've already divulged.

I'm warming up and stretching in the room Pollux and I have been training in. It smells damp in here today, and I'm fighting with my senses that are begging me to leave.

Pollux storms in, slamming the door behind him.

"What the fuck, El?" he growls.

"Uhm . . . I'm not sure what is happening? I think you're the one who is late?" I glance around the room, like there might be someone else to save me from this encounter.

There isn't.

"What. Is. This," Pollux snaps, holding up a feather.

"Uh, it looks like a feather?" I shrug.

"It was found in *your* room." He glares.

I stare at him. "Uhm, okay. You've been in my room before."

"This isn't *mine*. It's yours, and I know it. It smells like *you*," he snaps.

"Well, that is a very serious accusation. Do you have any evidence other than this supposed smell?" I ask.

"El, I know it's yours," he sighs. "Sometimes I wish you'd go back to being the quiet, reserved girl who showed up here. The one ready to tell us everything she knew."

"Well that's fucking rude," I seethe.

"Let's just get started . . ." he says. He walks over to the wall and takes his shirt off, and tosses it on the floor.

"Uh, what are you doing?" I look away quickly and divert my eyes.

"I'm going to shift with you today, since apparently you have an owl form," he states.

"I don't know what you're talking about." I look around the room, anywhere, other than at him. I do not want to see the contoured muscles of his chest.

One second, I'm trying not to look at Pollux, and the next second, Pollux is an owl.

The instant he shifts, I can feel the owl inside me raging to get out. Like it knows he is there, and wants to meet.

I push it down, groaning. I clench my teeth, my hands rolling into fists.

I fight, pushing it, while a bead of sweat trickles down my face.

I can't fight it much longer; my body aches, and the owl threatens to rip everything apart inside me.

The lights flicker, and my shoulders begin to hunch. The bones begin shifting beneath my skin. Feathers prick through my back, and burst in a soft rustle.

Pollux's golden eyes shine, locked on mine. I can feel the joy and pride beaming from him. Staring at him in his owl form, while I'm in my own, does something foreign to my body. I get this deep urge within me to be closer to him.

I can see the hunger and need in his eyes, too, and I immediately realize one of us needs to shift fast before our owl urges take over.

Heat fills my core.

My talons click across the hardwood floor as I move closer to Pollux. My feathers ruffle with desire.

I inhale, bones shift, and my skin reclaims me.

Pollux shifts too, and we stand there in our human forms, desire still burning in our eyes.

I blink rapidly, and take a deep breath.

"Sorry . . . I . . ." I start.

Pollux interrupts. "It's fine," he snaps, as he storms out of the room.

I'm laying in bed that night, comparing the book I just read about the Night Realm and the history of shifters, while trying to make sense of the map.

All the maps of the Night Realm are very different, and most are missing pieces, usually along the top. Like they've ripped off the same area of every copy on purpose.

In all my research over the past couple of weeks, I've found nothing about anyone who had multiple forms when shifting.

Although, I have learned that dragon shifters are rare, so rare that they typically automatically become royalty. If there is already a king who is a dragon shifter, then the newest dragon shifter must fight the current king to the death for the position.

I also haven't found a single record of a female dragon shifter either, but I know there has to be one somewhere. I can't possibly be the first one.

The past few weeks of training have flown by, and I haven't heard a single word from King Canis. When I asked, Atta she said he was no longer in the capital, and was away on business.

When I asked Pollux, he said, "Well, he's a busy man" and left it simply at that.

I place all the books and maps away on the dresser and climb into bed.

I stare up at the glass ceiling. The stars glow a pink hue tonight. As much as it pains me to admit, I am still enjoying the Night Realm. With the exception of the shifting, and possible betrothal, of course.

The stars still bring me a peaceful happiness, and I am happy to have a daily purpose that isn't just farming in the heat.

I close my eyes and try to force myself to sleep. Instead of sleep, though, my mind wanders to my training session with Pollux today. His heated gaze both in and out of his owl form.

A rush of heat runs down my spine. I shift uncomfortably in my plush bed.

His gaze lingers in my mind as I doze off . . .

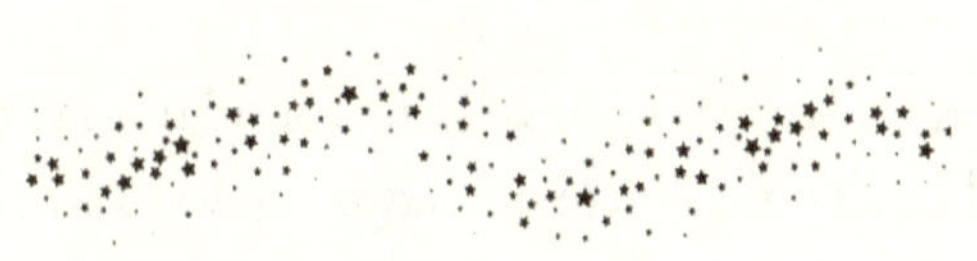

I glance up at Pollux. His lips quirk up in a smile. It's the first time I've seen him truly smile, and it's a gorgeous sight to behold.

He grabs my hands and pulls me to him. "You don't know how much I've wanted this," he whispers.

He pulls me closer, flush against him.

His breath is hot against my lips.

He starts to press his lips to mine, when a fog horn blows in the distance. We pull apart. Both of us staring out the open window.

Pollux shifts into his owl form and flies out the window.

I'm standing there alone, longing to go after him.

I wake covered in sweat, like I used to when I would dream of stars in Swaylin. Once again, it should feel good to have something that reminds me of home, but it doesn't. Life all feels like a blur at this point.

It's been a few weeks since I first found out I could shift. It feels like all my days are on a constant loop and all I do is eat, sleep, and train. Yet, none of my questions have been answered.

Am I engaged to be wed? Potentially the next queen?

I keep reading every bit of literature Atta will bring me about the Night Realm, but there is *a lot* redacted. There are a few lores about the shadow men, or dark creatures of the Night. I'm not sure if there is any truth to the stories, or if it's all just childhood folklore to keep the local kids away from the mountains.

Either way, I absorb all the information I can. Atta also brings me a few books for pleasure, once she realizes I love to read.

She quickly realizes I also love a good love story.

Atta comes in for the day. "I have great news, kid!"

"Oh, yeah?" I reply.

"Yep!" She grins. "You got yourself a day off! The king needs Pollux today, and he wants you to rest."

While this *should* feel like a gift, it brings the realization that I don't really know what to do with a day off.

I think for a minute. "Any chance anyone else has a day off?"

Atta grins.

"I haven't taken a day off in so long!" Atta smiles as we walk along the cobblestone streets of Canopus.

It's the first time I've ever seen her hair down and un-braided. Her fine black hair is mostly straight with the exception of a few small waves. Her green eyes shine extra bright today, with the reflection of the currently green stars in the sky.

She looks happy, although she usually is. Atta has such a unique presence. She's easy to trust, for whatever reason. Atta just says whatever she believes and doesn't sugarcoat reality. It's easy to trust and believe in someone who is always so brutally honest.

We walk up and down the streets of Canopus. We duck into a few shops, and Atta buys a soap from one.

"So, have you always lived in the Night Realm?" I ask her.

"I have not, but we moved here when I was young, so it's all I remember. My parents never shared where we were originally from." She slings the bag of soap over her shoulder, and cracks her neck.

"Did you always want to be part of the King's Guard?" I try to pry some more.

"Ha! Nope, not at all, actually. My parents both died tragically when I was around sixteen, and I was orphaned. I was forced to join the palace guard because that was the law for orphans over the age of thirteen at the time." She sighs. "But it worked out well for me, I have no complaints, things could always be worse."

I think for a minute. "When did you join the King's Guard? Before or after King Canis took over?"

She smirks. "So you have been reading all of those books." She laughs. "I joined the King's Guard prior to King Canis."

"So, are you a fan of the current king?" I glance at her.

She stops walking, and fully turns toward me.

"Elliora, don't ask questions like that in public. You never know who could be listening," she whispers.

We continue walking in silence.

After a couple more hours of walking and shopping, I ask Atta if there is anything else to do. She practically jumps with joy as she says, "I've been waiting for you to ask!"

She starts heading off back towards the palace. We are almost to the front doors when we run into Jaysen, Brock, and the two other girls from dinner at the start of my training.

Jaysen yells, "Hey! Elliora! Over here!" and starts waving aggressively.

Atta rolls her eyes, as I whisper to her, "Hold on, just one second."

I jog over to Jaysen. "Hey!" I awkwardly wave.

Jaysen smiles. "Hey you! Where have you been?"

"Oh, well, I got a day off today, so Atta was just showing me around the town since I haven't really seen it yet." Little does everyone know, I have seen it from the sky. I don't trust Jaysen, though, ever since the odd comment about my mother.

"That's awesome! We have the rest of the day off too! What are you guys going to do now?" he asks.

I glance over my shoulder at Atta, who has quietly moved closer. She sighs and says, "I guess he can come" with a grunt.

Jaysen's grin widens. "Where are we heading?"

Chapter Fifteen

ATTA TAKES US TO the stables to grab a few horses. She ties a covered wagon to her horse. We travel east to the base of the mountains, where she stops, and we all climb out of the wagon. Brock and the two girls, who I have learned *do* have names, Selene and Eos, have joined us. I don't think Atta is pleased with all of the people, but she hasn't commented on it.

I look up at the mountains. It's the first time I've seen snow up close.

The fresh snow blankets the tall mountain peaks like icing on a cake. Flurries drift lazily from the sky, glimmering in the starlight.

Jaysen, Brock, Selene, and Eos trudge through the powder, cheeks rosy, laughter echoing off the cliffs. I wonder what that feels like, to laugh freely with friends.

I look over at Atta, who pulls out a large basket. I run over to help.

"Thanks," she grunts.

We walk it over to a small hill where she lays out a gray checkered blanket on the snow. She sets the basket down and pulls out thermoses, sandwiches wrapped in wax paper, and a container of cookies.

The others come over, and we all sit down and begin munching. I'll never stop talking about how good the food is in the Night Realm.

Atta moans, "This is officially my best idea, ever."

I snort.

The others all chuckle, as Jaysen reaches for the tiny purple mugs Atta brought. "May I?" he asks her.

"Sure!" she grins.

Jaysen pours a hot chocolate drink into all the mugs. Steam curls into the cold, brisk air. Jaysen passes the mugs around until everyone has one.

I grip mine tightly and savor the warmth.

They all clink mugs and sip. Crumbs fall as they continue to dive into the food, and everyone is bundled up in thick jackets and beanies. After a while, the peaceful hush of falling snow surrounds us.

Suddenly, there is a soft thump—a snowball hits Jaysen square in the shoulder. He turns slowly to see Brock innocently sipping cocoa, eyes wide.

"Oh, it's *on*," Jaysen jests.

Jaysen lobs a snowball. Brock ducks—Selene takes the hit.

"Seriously?" Selene snips.

She dives for cover, scooping snow. The mountainside erupts into chaos. Snowballs fly. Laughter peals. Atta hides behind a snow-laden bush, forming perfect spheres with frightening speed.

Teams begin to form, and I find myself behind the bush with Jaysen and Atta. We are preparing for our final snowball attack on Brock, Selene, and Eos.

Eventually, everyone collapses into the snow, breathless and soaked, staring up at the dark night sky, and the glistening purple stars that decorate it.

"Next time," Eos mumbles, "we bring sleds."

They all nod, a chorus of agreement muffled by the falling snow.

I should feel scared, being in a strange place, surrounded by strange, new people. Instead, I just feel immense happiness.

It is late when we finally return to the palace. I take a warm bath, and cuddle into my blankets to read. I'm surprised to say, but I had an amazing day off.

When Atta told me this morning that I would need to rest and take the day off, I was truthfully dreading it.

I stare out the window of my room, and my mind wanders to Pollux. I wonder how his day was with the king.

I get out of bed, and move across the room to the open window, listening to the crisp breeze hum across the rooftops below.

I think about home, what my mom and grandpa would think if they could see me here, gazing at the stars outside. I think my mother was wrong: the stars are beautiful. They are silent witnesses to time's passage. The secrets they hold could probably answer all my questions and more.

There is a knock on the door, and I wrap the cozy black robe I've been wearing tighter around me. I pad across the room and swing the door open to see Atta with a tray of food for two.

"Figured we could end the night with some good food and—" She sets the tray down, and pulls her bag off her shoulder. "Some fun new books!"

She puts some new books down on top of my dresser.

"You're the best, Atta!" I grin.

"You're not so bad yourself, kid." She smiles back.

We spend the rest of the night eating and chatting about our lives before, both knowing we can never go back. When we finish eating, we sit and read together in comfortable silence.

It's the moment I realize, Atta is my first real friend.

Chapter Sixteen

Atta wakes me early the next morning.

She trains me on how to use a bow and arrow. Pollux is still off with the king somewhere, according to Atta.

I try to ask questions while we are training, but Atta just says, "I wish I could tell ya kid, I really do. Now quit holding the bow so tight. It looks like you're trying to strangle it."

I look down at my fingers. My knuckles are white around the riser.

"Oh, sorry. I just don't want to drop it," I mumble.

Atta laughs. "You won't drop it. Bows don't need force. They need balance. Try again, and relax your hand. Let the bow sit in your palm. Like this." Atta steps behind me and gently adjusts my fingers, guiding my posture. There's a practiced ease to her touch, neither rushed nor hesitant. It's a refreshing change of pace from my shifter training with Pollux.

Atta steps back and says, "Good. Now feet shoulder width apart. Left foot a little forward, and open your stance. Yes, like that!"

I shift on my feet, unsure about the placement, until Atta nods. "Yes, Ellie! Now draw with your back, not your arm. Think of your shoulder blades pulling together. Like you're pinching something between them."

I raise the bow, and draw the string shakily. The arrow trembles, and the tip wavers. "This feels unnatural and weird, Atta." I groan.

"It should. You're asking your body to move in a way it's never had to. But give it time, your body can learn fast if you let it." She beams, she looks so proud, and I know I'm going to let her down with this shot.

I exhale, and aim at the distant target. I release the arrow and watch as it arcs awkwardly and thuds into the dirt well short of the straw target.

I lower the bow, and frown. "That was terrible," I grumble.

Atta chuckles. "No. That was your first arrow. That makes it important. You'll never shoot another first arrow again."

I look at her surprised, because that's not what I expected her to say.

"Archery's not about force, Ellie. It's about patience, and precision. Think about the space between your

breaths. You don't fight the bow. You learn to listen to it."
She smiles.

I absorb her words, take a deep breath, and reach for another arrow.

"Good. Nock it, and this time, feel the string. Not just with your fingers, feel it with your whole body. Let the arrow go like a thought you're ready to lose." She speaks softly.

I think about what thought needs to leave my mind, and think about my dad. I think about how he somehow knows I'm here, and hasn't tried to see me anyway. I think about how every male face I've passed since arriving, I've examined with hope. It's left me feeling worthless, the fact he hasn't reached out. So, I take that thought... the thought that I'm worthless, and I let it go.

I draw again. This time, my motion is steadier. It's still imperfect, but more focused. I release.

The arrow sticks. It's off-center, but on the target.

It hit it. I smile.

I turn and look at Atta, and she gives the faintest smile. "Yes, Ellie! Now do it again!"

I groan, and she laughs, and we continue training.

The next day, she wakes me up early again, and we continue working on our archery skills. I get pretty decent. I can hit the target every time. Not on the center, but on the target consistently.

On the third day, Atta trains Jaysen, Brock, Selene, Eos, and a few others from Day Realm as well. We spend all morning working on fighting with a staff.

While I've been off training my shifting abilities with Pollux the past few weeks, it seems like the rest of the summoned have been training their weapon skills. Which only leads to more questions in my mind.

After a quick lunch break, Atta teaches us all how to wield a sword.

Atta stands before us, the rest of us stand in a semicircle.

"The sword doesn't care who you are. It doesn't care if you're strong, fast, or scared out of your skin. All it asks is that you respect it and understand it." She pauses a moment, and lets the words hang in the air. I love the way Atta explains weapons, but glancing at the group, I get the feeling Selene does not. "If you grip it too hard, it'll turn stiff in your hands. If you're too loose, it will fly away. You want control, but not brute force."

She demonstrates in a clean fluid motion. She guards, strikes, and recovers with the straw dummy before her.

"Now you try." She smiles.

She walks around and helps each of us individually with our stance.

Everyone is clumsy, but moving. She continues to work around the semicircle, helping each of us.

Eventually, we pause for a water break.

"This sucks," Selene grumbles. "I never thought I'd be training on weapons."

Eos nods her head in agreement.

When we start again, I ask, "Atta, How will we know if we're doing it right? I feel kind of silly still."

Atta demonstrates again, raising her blade again and cutting once, so fluid it barely seems to move, yet, the straw dummy is in half, and has dropped to the floor.

She smiles again. "When it feels like falling forward, like you aren't forcing it. Just let it drop where you guide it. The sword wants to move, let it."

We all try again, everyone getting a little bit better every time.

Jaysen and Brock high-five each other and yell.

Atta smiles at them. "Great! Now, again. Until your hands ache. Until your shoulders scream. Until you no longer need to think about how to stand. That's when the real work begins."

They both groan loudly, and Atta laughs.

Selene whines, "How long will that take?"

Atta looks at Selene. "Depends. How much do you want to be the one still standing when it ends?"

We fall into motion. We are awkward, but determined. A rhythm begins among us, clumsy but growing steadier with each cut. In the silence between strikes, you can hear the shape of discipline and teamwork forming.

On the fourth day, I get a note sent to my room that the king is making a proclamation for all of the Night Realm to hear. It asks that I urgently make my way to meet him.

I get dressed quickly, and open my door to find Atta and Pollux waiting for me.

Pollux looks breathtaking. His hair is tied into a low bun. His twin swords are sheathed and crossed across his back.

His face is stone-cold as always, but he has the smallest hint of a smile at the corner of his lips. Like he's relieved to see me, or maybe I can just tell from the creases in the corners of his eyes.

I smile up at him, and then smile at Atta. Atta looks worried, twisting her hands together in front of her.

I frown. "Are you okay?" I whisper.

She pulls her hands apart, and puts them behind her back. "Yep, never better." She smiles, and then turns and heads down the hallway.

Pollux gestures for me to follow. I sigh, and take off behind Atta. We make our way to the room I first shifted in.It seems to be a favorite room for the dear king.

Atta and Pollux stop at the door, and turn to look at me. Atta says, "He would like to speak to you alone before the . . . proclamation."

"Okay." I smile and act brave. Internally, I'm panicking. Although, I will say, knowing I have the ability to shift has given me a new level of confidence that I've never had.

Still, the king has shifted into a dragon . . . enough that he defeated the previous king. So I think I have every right to be nervous.

I take a deep breath, and open the massive doors.

I step into the elegant room, actually taking the time to observe my surroundings this time.

It's a large briefing room. A massive oak table in the center with a replica of the mountains, and valley where Canopus resides.

There is a large arched window on the far side of the room where King Canis currently stands with his back to me, looking out the window.

"Good Morning, Elliora dear, how have you been?" His nasally voice grinds on my every nerve.

I smile anyway. I've gotten pretty good over the past month at forcing smiles and making them appear real. At least, I think I have.

King Canis turns, and I answer. "Great, sir, how have you been?"

"Wonderful! Everything is exactly as it should be, finally." He claps his hands together and makes his way to the table.

He places both hands on either side of the largest mountain and leans over.

"Are you ready to wed, Elliora?" he asks.

I startle, but try to save it by placing my hand over my heart, like I'm joyous at the thought.

King Canis smiles. "Elliora, you don't need to fake anything. This is a marriage arranged by the gods and fate. You don't need to be pleased now, but I hope you will be pleased by the wealth and luxury it brings to you in the future."

I glance down at my feet, trying to think of the right words, but nothing feels right. There is nothing to say that wouldn't strain this relationship.

"I am excited about the idea of the future," I finally say. It's the only thing that's true, I've never been excited about my future before. Now, though, I have friends, I feel comfortable under the stars, and I am excited to see what the future holds for me. Maybe even where my dad resides . . .

He smiles. "Well, there you go. We will wed, as it was willed by the gods. You are the prophecy we have been waiting for. We will wed and together the Night Realm will prosper." He clasps his hands together and heads to the door.

"Elliora, it's almost time for our proclamation. Please have someone dress you appropriately for the occasion." He smiles, and exits the room.

I stand there and stare at the door.

This odd feeling fills my chest. It's a feeling I don't entirely know.

The door swings open, and Atta stands there. She stares at me for a long second, before coming over and grabbing my hand.

She gives my hand a squeeze in comfort, and takes me to get ready for the royal proclamation.

I'm to be dressed in finery.

The hush of the room is almost scary.

Stars, looking like diamonds, are scattered across the night sky, and peek through the tall windows. Outside this room, the courtyard murmurs with activity, but in here, time has slowed to a breathless pause.

I sit before the mirror. My gown—a cascade of midnight blue silk embroidered with silver thread—lies across the dresser, waiting for me. It shimmers faintly, like the surface of a calm sea under starlight.

People move around me in quiet harmony, their hands deft and sure. One pins my hair into a soft crown of waves, threading in strands of pearls and tiny crystal pins. Another kneels to slip satin slippers on my feet, whispering that the floor will feel like clouds beneath me.

But it is my own gaze in the mirror that holds the most weight. I'm not nervous, no, I've been secretly preparing for this. Beneath the surface is something electric. I have a secret hope, a buried fear, and a flicker of rebellion.

My corset gets tightened, and my dress slides on. My necklace is clasped around my neck, and the final touch—a ring, centuries old, passed from queen to queen—slides onto my finger. Destiny is a heavy thing to wear, even when it glitters.

I stand.

The bottom of my gown caresses the wooden floor. Everyone takes a step back to admire their hard work.

In that moment, just before the doors open, before the trumpets and courtiers begin to play . . . I am not just a future queen.

I am a storm in stillness. Ready as I'll ever be.

I step out onto the balcony with my betrothed, King Canis.

Chapter Seventeen

We stand on a balcony of the eleventh floor, overlooking the city of Canopus. The streets are packed full of every man, woman, and child who resides here.

"Good day, citizens of Canopus!" the king bellows into the crowd. It echoes off the pavement and glass buildings, at the crowd's utter silence.

"It is my joy and honor to present the future Queen of Night, Elliora Polaris!" he shouts. The crowd erupts into cheers. The king whispers, "Curtsy now," gruffly.

The crowd dims to quiet again as I curtsy.

The king begins again, "She is the one of legends, the one from the prophecy! She is here to help Night rise to its full potential, to bring us to the Summit of Shadows, and the Demise of Day!"

My head snaps to him. Where the fuck was this information earlier? What the hell is the Demise of Day?

The crowd cheers again, but not as loudly. I glance down, and all the summoners from the Day Realm aren't cheering. To be honest, I wouldn't cheer either if I just heard the words 'Demise of Day' come from this Night King's mouth.

I swallow, and take deep breaths. This corset is going to kill me standing this high up.

The king continues, "No longer will we be burdened by the terrors of the north. You now have not one, but *two* dragon shifters who will lead you into the Summit of Shadows. We have three weeks to prepare. Everyone will continue with their training. Our merchants need to start storing food, water, and paper goods needed for the war ahead. I believe that the battle against our northern enemy will pass quickly, and then we will have a break to prepare for the war ahead against Day."

The people shout and cheer again, and I feel like I'm going to be sick.

I've never heard of a single issue between Night and Day, especially not one that would warrant a whole damn war.

Day Realm and Night Realm have always disliked each other, but there was never an outright animosity as far as I could see. Our two realms have handled everything individually over the years.

This is the first I've ever heard about a possible impending war between them.

I clench my fists together, tampering down the rage simmering within me. I can see a dragon and a wolf ready to pounce at any second. I take deep breaths and push them down.

The skin on my arm starts to scale.

I rub it. King Canis turns briefly, and sees a scale.

He grabs my hand and pulls me up next to him. "Welcome to the Rise of Night! Begin the preparations we have been waiting for all these years."

He raises my hand up in the air with his, and the crowd roars.

He pulls me back inside through the doors. I try to pull my hand away, but he grips it harder. "What the fuck was that!" I shout.

He gently lifts my hand, kisses my knuckles, and then whispers, "See you soon, dear fiancée."

He strolls away with an elegance that irritates me.

I turn abruptly and run into Atta, her arms are crossed in front of her, like she's been impatiently waiting.

"Hey," I whisper.

"Can't say I love this whole queen look. I think I prefer your helpless little Swaylini look." She smiles.

I can tell she's trying to make light of the situation, but I don't smile. I feel like the solid plan I had formed in my head is crumbling after that speech.

She frowns. "Hey. It'll be fine, you have me." She reaches forward and grabs my hand.

In my nineteen years of existence, I've never known the comfort of someone just holding your hand. Before all of this, I'd never just held anyone's hand before. Jaysen, Atta, and even the king have all held my hand in an effort to try and comfort me since I arrived in the Night Realm.

It feels nice, but every time someone does, it feels foreign. Like it's a reminder that I don't know who I actually am, and that I feel as though I can't trust anyone.

I look down at where Atta's hand holds mine. It might be stupid, but I think she's the only one I truly trust. Maybe I shouldn't, but she feels the most real to me.

I look up at her. Her eyes are glossy, but she blinks a few times, and then smiles again.

"What do you want to do now?" She asks, "Eat our feelings in chocolate? Read some books? Take a walk outside?"

"All of the above," I mumble.

"Great," she says. We walk in silence through the hallway back to my room. We turn the corner, and I run straight into this funny short man I feel like I should know, and the kid from the eleventh floor.

I'm trying to place the short man in my mind. *Where do I know him from?*

"Miss Elliora." He bows.

"Ah, yes, uhm . . . " I stutter. I'm entirely uncomfortable with his bow, and cannot figure out how I know him.

"Tate, or Taterfall," he reminds me, "the chef from your ship here to the Night Realm." He smiles at me.

That is it, yes. He said he knew my dad? "Oh yes, right! Tate, I apologize sincerely. The boat feels like a lifetime ago now. Time passes quickly here in Night."

I glance at the guy next to him . . . Arcturus, he said his name was. He was the odd one who spoke to me in the food line.

"Sure. Well, I'm here in the palace cooking for a few days, if you ever—" Tate glances at Atta, and then back at me, "need anything." He bows again and then limps off.

Arcturus nods his head at me, and then follows closely behind.

When he is out of earshot, Atta turns to me. "Well, that was *odd*."

I stare at the place where they just stood. I have so many questions. Questions for the king, Tate, Arcturus, and even for Pollux, but most importantly, I have a million questions for my dad.

I wonder again, if I will ever find him. Will I ever even know who he is? Does he know where I am?

All of my questions will have to wait, though. I shake my head, and shake it off. "Alright, let's get to my room already. I want out of this dumb gorgeous gown. This corset is currently threatening to kill me."

Atta laughs so hard she snorts. "You got it, kid. Let's move."

I finally get the corset and gown off. Atta suggests that following the proclamation I keep my head low and wear a hood. She fashions a large black scarf she has into a hooded wrap. Once she decides I look hidden enough, we spend the rest of the afternoon strolling the streets of Canopus.

When we return to the palace, I make my way to the dining hall for dinner. While Atta does . . . whatever the hell Atta does.

Dinner is quieter than usual. There is a hush as soon as I enter the dining hall, but I ignore it and scan the room for Jaysen. I find him near his usual spot, waving at me wildly.

I smile, and walk over.

He's with Brock, Selene, and Eos. I sit down at the table as someone brings me a platter of food. I make eye contact with the server and say, "Thank you!"

They nod their head and walk away.

Selene, Brock, and Eos all stare at me, waiting. "Did I miss something?" I say.

Selene answers, "Uh, no. Just wondering when you were going to tell us you're going to be queen and kill all of our families?"

Her tone is harsh and bitter, but I don't blame her one bit.

Eos, Selene, and Brock give me menacing glares.

I glance around the tables. The surrounding people are also giving me unforgiving looks.

Meanwhile, Jaysen just politely smiles at me, like I'm the same Elliora that got on the ship in Swaylin.

I look at Selene specifically. "Well, I didn't know until about fifteen seconds before you that I was going to be queen, and I didn't know until the *exact* moment you did that I'm supposedly some death sentence for us all. The only thing I knew for sure was that I developed the ability to shift. Other than that, though, it turns out I'm as clueless as you are." I smile, before taking a huge bite of potatoes.

They taste different tonight, but it could very well be the events of today playing tricks on me.

Jaysen reaches over and rubs my shoulder before patting it gently. I glance over at him and smile. I wish I could trust Jaysen. It would be nice to have a friend other than Atta that I could rely on, but I can't shake the feeling that his comment about my mother means something more. Right now, though, he provides me with a comforting presence that I can't help but want amongst the chaos.

I continue to eat while Selene and Eos start whispering between themselves. Brock and Jaysen start talking about training plans for tomorrow.

Apparently, while I've been off training my shifting abilities, they've been following a strict training plan to prepare them for war.

The meat tonight is delicious, is the last thought I have before I fall face first into my potatoes.

I wake up in my bed to yelling. Pollux and Atta yell at each other on either side of my bed. Jaysen sits in the chair at the corner and immediately jumps up when he sees my eyes open.

"Elliora! Thank the gods!" He comes rushing over, and grabs my hand. "Are you okay? How are you feeling?"

I'm disorientated and trying to catch up with what just happened. The last thing I remember is, I . . . "Did someone fucking poision me?" I shout.

Pollux moves his terrifying glare from Atta to me, and then softens ever so slightly the moment our eyes lock. "Unfortunately, yes. Everyone is currently locked in the dining hall while we figure out who is responsible and what the fuck happened. Well, *almost* everyone." Pollux shifts his gaze to Jaysen.

"I wasn't staying there! I needed to make sure she was okay!" he yells.

Atta sighs.

"Boys, we've already been over this. She's awake now, so everyone can calm down. The doctor's potions worked exactly how she said they would."

She leans down and whispers to me, "Do you want me to make them leave?"

"Over my dead body," Pollux grits out.

Atta raises her eyebrows at him in question.

"The king would not want me to leave anyway," he mumbles.

"Sure, right," Atta says. "Well, whatcha think my sweet little Ellie, wanna read and hang out?" She grins at me.

"Yeah, for sure, grab the books." I smile back at her.

She runs over to the dresser and pulls out a stack. She brings them back and places them along the foot of my bed.

She takes off her shoes, and then removes all her leathers and weapons, placing them all on the nightstand. She climbs into the bed with me and I giggle.

Pollux grunts, and then says, "What in all the realms do you think you're doing, Atta?"

"The same thing Ellie and I have been doing, reading . . . comfortably. Cause that's the best way to read." She smiles at him, before finding her comfy position and beginning to read.

We've been doing this quite a bit the past couple of days, reading literature cozy in my room. It's very quickly become the highlight of my life here, and quite possibly, the best thing I've ever done with another person.

"Aren't you on duty?" Pollux seethes.

"I am not. I am currently just a friend." Atta smirks at him, before continuing to read.

She's currently reading a love story about a princess locked in a tower who falls in love with her bodyguard.

Meanwhile, I've been researching the history of royalty in the Night Realm, and the first shifters to appear. It's a lot of the same information, but I still can't find a previous female who could shift into a dragon.

There is usually only one male dragon shifter alive at any given time, because they fight to the death for the position of king when another comes along. In the recorded history, there is only one instance of two male dragon shifters being alive at the same time. And it didn't last for long before the ascended king assassinated his opponent.

The only other information I can find pertaining to shifters is a hierarchy of sorts. Owls typically come in behind dragons, which I find odd. I glance at Pollux. I'd love to ask him why owls seem to come second in rank, but I know I can't ask here with Jaysen around.

Behind owls are larger cats: lions, tigers, panthers. That one makes more sense to me.

I keep flipping the pages, hoping to find something more, to find something that sticks out as unusual. Nothing comes though. I slam the book closed.

Pollux and Jaysen end up sitting in the chairs, I glance over to see Pollux with his brooding stare, and Jaysen with his downright puppy dog smile.

"Do you guys want some books to read? If you're just going to linger over there anyway?" I smile at them.

"Sure!" Jaysen says happily. "I haven't had a chance to read since we were back home." He gets up and crosses the room to sift through the available books. He ends up picking up a book about star patterns, which I immediately take note of.

Pollux doesn't say a word, but comes over and grabs a book titled, *Shifters in Flight*. I've read that one already. It discusses the typical traits and abilities of shifters who can fly.

I grab a new book too, another book on the history of shifters.

We all sit in silence for a while, reading. Occasionally, someone will come up and trade their book for another. Atta eventually cuddles close to me as the temperature drops, and Pollux's nostrils flare at the sight.

She chuckles.

We continue reading until there is a loud pounding at the door. Atta is on her feet with her leathers back on and weapons drawn before Pollux even gets the door open.

A tall, dark, muscular man on the King's Guard who I've seen interact with Pollux and Atta before begins whispering to Pollux. I'm trying to place him in my mind . . . he's that same lion shifter. I still don't know his name, but he was the one who realized I was in the room when I first shifted.

There is clearly a hierarchy of some kind amongst the shifters, beyond what it said in my book.

Pollux nods his head, and then glances at me.

His hands clench into fists at his sides.

I whisper over to Atta, "What's his name?"

"Regulus" Atta whispers back.

"Great, thank you for the update," Pollux says to Regulus. He then nods his head in dismissal at him.

Pollux looks to Atta. "The poison came from a chef with ties to an enemy. They just wanted Elliora dead for strategic purposes."

"Is that supposed to make me feel *better*?" I snap.

They both glance at me, and then back at each other, ignoring me. "Under the king's orders, Elliora is to stay in her room until further notice. Food will be sent to her after inspection by those reliable to the king. She is not to leave the room until the king has given approval."

"So, what, I'm a prisoner now?" I groan.

"No, you're under supervision until we know you are safe. Your safety comes first," Pollux demands.

I huff out a sigh, and cross my arms over my chest. I glance to Jaysen sitting in the corner still.

"Eh, I have to agree, Elliora, I want you safe and healthy." He smiles.

Whatever.

"Okay, great, well that's just perfect." I flop back onto the bed. I look up at the stars, and it immediately calms me. I can feel my heart rate slow in my chest.

My eyes water. The emotions flood my chest and I want everyone out of this room before I completely break down.

As if Atta can sense my thoughts, she says, "Boys, why don't you turn in for the night? I'll take the first watch of Elliora. You guys go get some rest. I have a feeling the king will want eyes on her from now on."

Pollux nods. "Yeah, I got the sense he will demand that first thing in the morning." He looks at Atta. "You sure you don't need to rest first?"

"I'm good." She smiles at him.

Jaysen yawns. "Alright, well, I'm glad you're okay, Elliora. I'll come check on you tomorrow if I'm allowed?" He shifts his eyes at Pollux, before looking back at me.

He briskly leaves the room.

When the door shuts behind him, Pollux grunts, "I don't trust that *kid*." He spits the word kid out like an insult. I roll my eyes.

I'm laying on the bed, and Pollux hesitates for a second, before saying "Goodnight, Elliora" and leaving the room.

Atta takes off her weapons and leathers again, this time placing them in the chair Pollux was sitting in before.

She climbs into bed with me, before saying, "Let it out, kid. Let it out."

And I cry.

I cry more than I ever have before.

I can't explain why.

I just sob. I thought about that moment, was it a few days ago? Or a few weeks ago now? I don't know anymore, time has blurred in the Night Realm. But I think about the moment I thought about drowning myself in that bathtub, and I wish I had.

So I cry some more.

Chapter Eighteen

I WAKE UP WITH no concept of time. There is breakfast and lunch on the table, and Atta sits in a chair, reading.

"Morning, sleepy head. There is some food here for you."

She says nothing of my complete meltdown the night before. She never asked why I was crying or tried to make it better. She was just there.

I won't lie, I've never cried in front of another person before.

I thought I'd wake up embarrassed or feeling even worse, but I don't.

I wake up feeling reborn.

I walk over and sit with her, and begin snacking on some of the food in front of us. "Still reading the same book?" I gesture to the book in her hands.

"Nah, I've moved on to the sequel. It's *so* good, you should read it sometime. It's beautifully written."

"Maybe I will someday." I smile at her.

Sometimes I wonder what life would've been like if I had a friend like Atta back home. Someone who was just always there for me, and didn't judge me. Someone I could talk about the stars with, and not feel scared.

Life would probably look much different.

"Any specific food requests? I think Pollux is going to come make me trade shifts with him soon, and I can try and get a word in with the chef while I'm gone?" She stands, and stretches.

"I think I'm okay." I smile. I think about asking her for some of the delicious chocolate we had the other night, but I feel like I'm already a burden. I'll just keep things easy.

"Okay!" she says. She goes and pulls out clothes for me and sets them in the bathroom.

I hear her turn the shower on before coming out.

"I would shower and change before Pollux gets here, or someone will worry." She laughs.

"Do I smell that bad?" I chuckle.

"No, but we don't want to cause any more concern than we already have." She comes over and fully embraces me in a tight hug.

"Go on. Get in the shower. I'll wait right outside the door to your room until Pollux gets here, give you the small amount of privacy I can." She gestures to the bathroom.

I stare at her face, her pale skin, her green eyes sparkling in the starlight. She has been nothing but wonderful to me, and I think about telling her right now.

But the words don't come out. I quietly mumble "Thanks" before heading into the bathroom.

I take a long shower. Honestly, what else is there to do today if I end up being stuck prisoner in my room?

Eventually, I dry off, with the towel wrapped around me still. I stare at the clothes Atta left out for me to wear . . . but what is the point? I can't leave my room.

I put them away and put on dark purple silk pajamas instead.

I decide to braid my wet hair and climb back into bed.

I watch the stars twinkle above. I used to force myself back home to pick one thing every day to feel grateful for. With so many things making life miserable, it always helped to focus on something good.

Today I'm grateful my room is on the top floor, so I can still see the stars.

I spend some time watching the stars, the various ways they seem to sparkle. One by one, patterns emerge like old friends I haven't seen in years.

Last night, one of the books I read said, the stars are stories. That they've been watching us longer than we've known how to look back.

What do the stars above me right now say? Will they offer me guidance for the journey to come? Or just provide the comfort I've grown to love?

I close my eyes for a moment. I don't know what tomorrow will bring, but for now, the universe is still, and I am a part of it.

I roll over on my side and glance at the window. I sit up abruptly as a thought crosses my mind . . . I could open that window and fly off.

Why haven't I thought of this sooner?

I walk across the room and fling open the window.

I place my hands on the windowsill and gaze out at the sky. The cool breeze hits my face, calling to me, taunting me . . .

The door to my room swings open, and Pollux's golden eyes find mine instantly.

"El, don't," he seethes.

"I'm not going to, but I was considering it." And that's the truth. I did consider flying away, I still am if I'm being honest. I wouldn't fly away in front of him, though. That would be downright stupid.

I look back out the window towards the Northern Mountains. The breeze picks up, and I shiver. I turn around and climb back into bed.

"So, that's it? Back to bed already?" Pollux asks.

"What else is there to do? I'm stuck in here . . . aren't I?" I snap.

Pollux's face softens. "Hopefully not for much longer." He sighs.

There is a sharp knock at the door, and Pollux leaves to get it.

After a moment, voices start to rise. I leap out of bed and head for the door to see what the commotion is.

Tate is at the door with a small brown package in his hand. The thread around it was tied with a bow, and the envelope on top has my name written in script.

"What's this?" I gesture to the package.

Tate smiles. "Oh, it's for you, Miss Elliora." He tries handing me the package.

Pollux steps in the way, placing himself between us.

"It needs to be checked before you accept it," he grunts.

"Oh, nonsense! It isn't poison right, Tate?" I smile at him.

"No. It isn't." He grins back at me.

Tate is short, but he has a charm to him. He instantly makes you feel safe. I grab the package from him, and open the letter.

Scrawled in ink, the letter reads: "Dearest Elliora, I can't wait to meet you -Dad"

I read the card again and again, because surely, my dad is not so close to send a present, but not come say hi himself?

I hold the package in my hands, I wish I could say I've spent my whole life wondering about him. But honestly, I only just started wondering what he may be like after the Dark Crossover.

Do I have his laugh? Or his temper?

There have been days here in the Night Realm, I catch myself looking in the mirror, studying the slant of my eyebrows or the shape of my eyes. They are not like my mom's. Maybe they are like his? And I wonder: *Did he ever think about me? Did he ever stop mid-step and wonder what age I might be now, what I might look like, or if I have his stubbornness?*

I glance back to the package in my hands. It trembles under my touch. I open the brown paper wrapping to find a book, titled *Gods and Goddesses of Andromeda*.

"Andromeda?" I say out loud. I glance at Pollux, whose face has gone pale. Tate has disappeared. I step out into the hallway, and look both ways, but he is long gone.

I turn back around as Pollux grabs me and hurls me inside my room, slamming the door behind me.

"Hide it," he shouts.

"What?" I ask.

"I said, hide it! Quick!" he shouts again.

I glance around the room, I walk over to the bed, lift up the mattress, and place the book under it. I look back at Pollux. "Why the hell do I need to hide it?" I question.

"If . . . if the king knew you had that," he pauses, "we'd be dead."

Chapter Nineteen

Eventually, I got Pollux to calm down and convinced him to stand guard outside the room. He protests a lot . . . especially since he knows I can shift into an owl.

I promised I just wanted a long bath, and didn't want him in here for that.

That was a lie, though. I wanted to read this book.

The book has a few chapters on the Goddess Hemera, the Goddess of Day, who I learned a lot about in Swaylin. It also has chapters on the Goddess Nyx, who is supposedly the Goddess of Night. It's interesting, I haven't seen a single thing about her in any of my readings here.

There are also chapters on the God Astraeus, the God of Dusk, and the Goddess Asteria, the Goddess of Stars.

Towards the end of the book, there is one chapter on a God named Erebus. It is said he is the God of Darkness and Shadows.

The final chapters summarize something called "The Great Awakening" and "The Great Divide."

The Great Awakening explains the beginning of Andromeda. A land created by the gods and goddesses themselves. There is a small sketched map that somewhat resembles what I know to be the Day Realm and the Night Realm. However, it has much more land on it that I am unfamiliar with. There are symbols across it. A sun, a moon, a cloud, and a darker, more misty cloud.

I want to make notes in a journal, but it feels too risky after Pollux said we could die for the possession of this book.

I skip ahead because I feel like I'm running out of time to claim that I'm bathing. I finally reach the part about "The Great Divide."

The legend says the Goddess Nyx left the God Erebus for another, and Erebus erupted into darkness. That darkness and mist encircled the world and filled every crevice and home. Goddess Hemera poured every ounce of her magic into ridding the darkness that covered their world, but could only cover what is now known as Swaylin.

There is a hard knock on the door. I jump, and shove the book back under the mattress. The door opens, and a chef walks in with a tray of food, followed by a brooding Pollux. The chef sets the tray down gently on the table, nods his head at me, and leaves the room.

Pollux gestures to the tray. "Please eat, so the king doesn't come here and bite my head off for your lack of nutrition," he grumbles, and then turns to leave the room.

"Wait!" I shout.

Pollux turns toward me. "Stay and keep me company?" I ask.

I immediately hate that I asked, it makes me seem needy and immature. I shouldn't need company, and I should be able to eat alone.

A minute that feels like a century passes, and Pollux nods his head once, and then takes a seat in one of the two chairs in the sitting area.

I walk over and sit across from him, while picking at the food on the tray. It looks like another delicious spread of meats, cheeses, fruits, and veggies. I pick up a carrot and look at it. "Where do you get produce in the Night Realm? Is it grown here?"

"I actually don't know. I guess I've never thought about it," he replies.

I smile, and continue to munch on the carrot. The crunching noises make the silence unbearable and awkward.

I try to think of something to talk to him about. "When did you first realize you could shift into an owl?" I ask.

"When I turned fifteen, my brother shifted for the first time. My parents were so disappointed I didn't shift as well. Two weeks later, both of my parents died in a tragic accident, and I shifted after their funeral." His voice is filled with hollow memories and sorrow.

"I'm so sorry for your loss," I whisper. "I know those words don't mean a whole lot, but truly I'm very sorry you had to experience that . . ."

"It's in the past. When are you going to tell people you can shift into anything you want?" he questions.

I glance at him. "Who says I can shift into *anything*?"

"Well, it's currently just a hunch. I've only heard of one other person in this world who had the ability to shift into more than one living being, and they could shift into anything . . . or at least, it seemed like they could. I guess I wouldn't know for sure. I know for sure of at least six things they could shift into." He raises an eyebrow at me in question.

"What were the six beings?" I ask.

"Hmm, there was a tiger, snake, owl, cat, wolf, and dragon that I know of." He glances at me again, with the same questioning look. "What have you shifted into?"

"What makes you think there is anything more than you've seen?" I keep my face as stiff and unfazed as possible.

"I knew the moment you made the dark crossing that you were extraordinary. I could feel it in my soul, like a great awakening. You've continued to exceed my expectations in every way. There is not a doubt in my mind you are the one from the prophecy, the one who can be themself in any form." His eyes lock on mine.

Those golden eyes that sparkle in my dreams. The eyes that I swear I've known my whole life.

I don't answer him, though. Instead, I shove a bread roll in my mouth and smile. "What does this prophecy say anyway?" I ask.

He opens his mouth to answer when there is a series of knocks on the door. Pollux stands and goes to answer. Atta walks in, and throws herself into the chair Pollux was just sitting in.

"What did I miss?" she asks with a grin, while handing me the box of chocolates I was dreaming about asking her for earlier today.

Chapter Twenty

I SHOWED ATTA THE book, Pollux eventually left, and Atta and I stayed up late reading again. Or at least I think it was late? It's almost harder to tell what time it is here in the Night Realm, or maybe it's just because I've been sleeping so much lately.

I finally get the all clear to leave my room the next day, but I have to be escorted by a member of the King's Guard in order to do so.

I spend the next few days in another series of training, eating, and sleeping. My book is still wedged under my mattress, untouched.

I've got the small start of a plan to get out of marrying the king, but in order to accomplish it, I need to train *hard*.

My body aches from all the shifting and training I've been doing. I'm exhausted after every shift, and need to prepare my body for the endurance it will need to move forward.

Pollux has warmed up some since our meal together. I think I even saw him smile in one of our training sessions, although he masked it quickly with a growl.

You'd think he shifted into a tiger or wolf the way he prowls and growls all the time. Though, when he's observing something, you can see the owl-like stillness he possesses.

I'm in my bath, soaking my sore muscles. Atta is in the other room preparing for another night with me. I haven't been trusted alone at all since the other night. I think Pollux confirmed his suspicions and reported to someone that I shouldn't be alone. So Pollux has been on duty during the day to train me and make sure I'm eating. And Atta has been on duty at night to make sure I'm sleeping.

While Atta is fun to be with, I'd love a night alone. I need some time alone to continue to formulate a plan. I trust Atta completely, but as a member of the King's Guard, she has to have some kind of commitment or loyalty to the king.

What I have planned would be considered treason. Therefore, Atta cannot be in on it, at least not until I know where she lies one hundred percent.

As I sit in the bath, I can't help but consider drowning again. It would end my problems quickly and easily, and who would really even miss me?

Atta shouts, "You almost done in there? I'm ready for the extra warmth in this damned bed!"

I laugh; apparently Atta would miss my body heat, so I guess I'll wait another day before I off myself.

I climb out and dry myself off.

I've gotten pretty used to life here. How long have I even been in Night Realm now? I would honestly enjoy living here so much if it wasn't for a damn prophecy and a wedding to the king.

Once I'm dressed, I braid my thick strawberry-blonde hair to the side. I walk out into the bedroom. Atta is sprawled out on the bed reading another book. The starlight seeps through the windows, and I go to climb into bed, when the door swings open and a brooding Pollux storms in.

He looks straight at Atta. "This is our chance. The guards rotate in fifteen minutes. One quiet sprint to the stables, and after that it's freedom."

Atta glares back at him. "And death if we're caught. We're not rats fleeing a cellar, Pollux. This is the royal palace. We will be fine here."

"What about El? Is she fine here, Atta? Remember the stories from your youth, not the lies we are currently being fed!" Pollux whisper-shouts. Keeping his voice low, but utter anger and loathing seeping through.

"What in Hemera is going on? Someone fill me in," I interrupt.

Atta gets out of bed, stepping closer to Pollux. Voice urgent but soft, she says, "Are you sure you want to do this tonight, Pollux? Are you *really* ready to stop playing their game, for her?" She points towards me.

"Atta, you said it yourself! This place is a prison with golden walls. She was never going to rule here, and she was going to be married off like a pawn." He grits his teeth.

"Excuse me, I'm still right here? Are we breaking out of here? What's going on?" I shove myself in between them, demanding answers.

Pollux turns to me. "What's out there is terrifying, but it's yours. In here? You already know your future. It ends with someone else writing your story. What do you want, El?"

I take a deep breath. "I want to write my own story."

Pollux smiles, and looks to Atta. "Astraeus, help us," she mutters.

I find it odd she is praying to the God of Dusk, but I don't have time to ask questions.

Atta looks at me. "Get whatever you need, quickly."

I turn to look at Atta. "Are you sure you want to do this? This is your home. You don't have to go if you don't want to?" My eyes water slightly at the thought of leaving Atta, but we both need to do what's best.

She smiles. "Nah, Ellie. I will go where you go."

Pollux grins triumphantly. Atta looks away, cursing as she begins to pack up her belongings. She's been bringing a bag here every night she has stayed, and I begin to wonder if she was waiting for this moment. She throws the book she was just reading into her bag.

All three of us begin to prepare in silence, the weight of the moment sharpening with each breath.

I grin wide: tonight, I'm writing my own damn story.

I throw the book from my dad and the wedding ring into my bag.

The faint sound of footsteps echoes in the hallway beyond my door. Pollux has his ear pressed to the door, while Atta gathers a small satchel she had hidden under my bed. Pollux checks his weapons, counting each one twice, and double-checking he has all he needs for the road ahead.

Pollux whispers to Atta, "There are two guards outside. They'll move in ten minutes, same as always."

Atta whispers back nervously, "If we make it to the stables, how far are we traveling? Do you have a plan?"

"We head north, to the border of The Great Divide. My contact will be waiting at the border, his name's Leon. He doesn't trust easily, so when we do get there, let me talk."

"You're awfully confident for a man who's betting his life on some mists and a friend," Atta mumbles.

"Confidence is the only thing that can get us out of here alive." Pollux stares at her, and then glances at me. "You ready, El?"

"Yes," I whisper.

He opens the door a sliver, and peeks out into the hallway. "See that? They're turning, it's the same route every night. We have five minutes with no eyes on this area. Let's move."

We move into the hallway and go the opposite direction I'm used to. Pollux opens a door, and we all move in. He closes the door behind us. We seem to be in a stairway. The only light being from the stars above.

Pollux grunts, "Move quickly, quietly, and carefully."

We all begin to make our way down the stairs as carefully as possible. It's so quiet you can hear every footstep. A noise echoes from down below, and we all freeze.

A tense silence falls as we wait; the ticking of Atta's wrist device sounds as loud as a yell right now. I hold my breath.

Pollux holds his hand up in a gesture that I assume means it's clear to keep moving, as they both start moving down the stairs again.

We make it to the bottom quickly, and quietly. Pollux stands at the door, which I assume takes us out of the palace. His ear pressed against it.

"Let's go," he whispers, and we move in unison through the doorway.

We turn a corner and—I run straight into Jaysen.

"Jaysen?" I whisper.

"Elliora, what are you doing?" He looks at me, and then at Pollux, and then at Atta.

"Are you . . . escaping?" he shouts.

Faster than I can even process, Pollux grabs Jaysen by the throat and lifts him into the air. "You will be quiet, or I will kill you right here and now. Do you understand?" Jaysen tries to speak but can't.

"Put him down, you big brute!" I whisper, smacking Pollux's arm.

Pollux drops Jaysen to the floor. Gasping for air, Jaysen mutters, "I'm coming with you."

"Like hell you are." Pollux groans.

"Jaysen, you don't even know where we are going," I whisper.

"We. Don't. Have. Time. For. This," Pollux seethes.

"How are you getting out of here? Horse? Flying?" he whispers.

Pollux sighs. "Horse."

"Great, I'll meet you at the stables. I'm grabbing my bag." He turns to leave.

"Are you sure you want to do this?" I ask.

While Pollux mutters, "If you don't make it, we will leave without you."

Jaysen turns. "Yes," he says to me, and "Okay," he salutes to Pollux.

I can tell the salute annoyed Pollux, but he shakes it off and turns to Atta and me. "Let's keep moving."

We make our way through the hallways and out the back door. As soon as we are out the door and into the crisp night air, we run into a guard. I don't recognize him, but Atta stiffens at the sight of him.

Before he can even say anything to us, Pollux slices his throat.

I shriek, and Atta grabs me and covers my mouth. Blood pools around him as his limp body falls to the ground with a soft thud.

Pollux wipes the blood off his blade and onto the long, dark cloak he is wearing.

I'm in a state of shock. Atta whispers in my ear, "Stay silent, Ellie."

She lets go of my mouth now, and I gasp for air. Not because she was suffocating me, but because I can't believe there is a dead guard in front of me.

Did he have a family? Did he deserve this?

"Keep moving," Pollux demands.

I push the thoughts down, deep inside me. I don't have time to think about this now. I gag a little, as we step over the puddle of blood that has now formed.

We make our way out towards the stables. It's similar to the way I walked to the Coliseum before. Which feels like months ago now, honestly, it feels like a different lifetime. So much has happened since then.

We keep running to the stables, and reach the outer courtyard. My heart is racing. The stables loom ahead, they look quiet, dark, and unguarded.

Pollux hurls open the door. The stables are dimly lit, with flickering torchlight. We hug the walls of the stables, I follow Pollux and Atta.

"Something's wrong. Where is the stable hand?" Atta whispers.

I glance around.

"I told him to leave the gate unlocked and disappear for a night. Paid him in gold. Let's hope he's greedy and not loyal," Pollux states, and we keep moving.

We reach a massive white horse with the name marker Pegasus. Pollux quietly opens the gate and starts untying the horse.

Atta keeps moving toward a large black horse named Epona. She begins untying it.

"What should I do?" I whisper to them.

"Nothing, just stand guard, we are only taking our own horses," Pollux whispers.

"What will I ride?" I ask.

"You'll ride with me," he says.

Pollux and Atta move their horse out of the back of the stables, when Jaysen comes running up behind.

"Oh, good. You made it," Pollux says snarkily.

Jaysen smiles at him. "Only two horses? Do you want me to get two more?"

"No, ride with Atta." He nods towards Epona.

"Or I can ride with Elliora, and you can ride with Atta," Jaysen snaps.

"Or I can kill you right now," Pollux grumbles.

"Stop. We don't have time for this," Atta seethes. "Get on my damn horse before I change my mind and leave you, Jaysen."

"Fine." Jaysen puts his backpack all the way on as Atta jumps up on the horse. Jaysen climbs up behind her and wraps his hands around her waist.

Pollux mounts Pegasus, scoots back, and tells me to climb in front of him.

I hesitate for a second, and look back at the palace.

I loved it there, but this *feels* right.

"Goodbye, gilded cage," I whisper.

I trust Atta. I'm not sure if I should, but I do. In my gut, this feels like the right thing to do. I look back at Pollux and grab his hand. He lifts me up onto Pegasus.

Pollux looks at Atta. "Ride hard, no heroics. Don't stop until I say."

"Right behind you," Atta says.

They spur their horses, and we gallop off towards the mountains. Behind us, the palace is silent and unaware.

Chapter Twenty-One

I'M SEATED IN FRONT of Pollux, his arms loosely around my waist, the horse's steady footsteps swaying us in sync. The starlight casts a warm glow over the trail, and the scent of dirt and leather mingles in the air. I lean back just slightly. I can't hold myself upright anymore. We've been riding for a couple of hours now in silence. It feels like everyone is too scared to speak right now. I've leaned back enough that I can feel Pollux's warmth through my shirt. I can hear the soft sound of his breath, and every once in a while, he turns his head as if he wants to say something, but he doesn't. The closeness feels intimate.

Our shared balance on Pegasus becomes a quiet dance. We move together with every step he takes, the rhythm creating an unspoken closeness between us. I'm not just holding on for balance anymore, I'm holding on because it feels good to be that close to him.

The dark trail finally opens to a mountainside, and Pegasus climbs steadily until we are overlooking a view that takes my breath away. Straight ahead are rolling snowy meadows, the sky painted in hues of purple and a diamond-like starlight.

We all pause there, still on our horses, still in silence, but the wind begins brushing softly against me.

After a moment of taking in the view, we continue on. The trail narrows slightly, and Pegasus carefully makes his way through a cluster of snowy trees, the starlight dimming under the canopy. We're still riding close, his arms resting lightly around me, but something in the air shifts, like the hush before a storm. We haven't spoken in hours, but I can feel the tension in his arms, a quiet withdrawal.

He leans forward slightly, voice low in my ear. "Can we talk?"

I hesitate, then nod. "Yeah. But it feels odd. Doesn't it?"

We both laugh lightly.

For a minute, it's just the creak of the saddle and the soft clop of hooves on the ground. "So what do we do now?" I ask Pollux, turning my head slightly, feeling his warm breath against mine.

He sighs. "We keep riding. We figure it out. Together."

Pegasus crests the next hill, and the snowy forest opens back up into the starlight. The trail stretches ahead, long and winding, but clear now. Pollux adjusts his grip around me, not tighter, just steadier.

And we ride on in more silence, neither of us quite sure what words to say.

After another thirty minutes of riding, we finally stop and take a break.

I hop off Pegasus and walk to the edge of the frozen river in front of us. I stretch every muscle I can. Jaysen comes up next to me, and it seems we have all decided it's finally safe to talk.

"Hey," Jaysen says quietly.

"Hi," I reply.

He smiles at me, and then begins stretching himself. Atta and Pollux pull out a map and start planning the next stretch.

Jaysen leans over and bumps his shoulder against mine. "This is crazy huh? Do you know where we are heading?"

"North." I shrug. "That's all I know."

"Hm, and why did we flee the castle? I mean, I would've followed you anywhere, but like, why did we leave?" he asks.

I think for a second. "I wanted to write my own story. I don't want to be Queen of the Night Realm, and be chained to King Canis. At least, not the way it was going to happen. I want to love someone when I get married." I sigh. "And I don't want to be treated as a pawn."

Pollux and Atta start walking over, and Jaysen turns towards them.

"Horse riding sucks, why aren't we flying?" he asks Pollux.

Pollux raises an eyebrow at him. "Can you shift into a flying creature that I am unaware of?"

"Well . . . no," Jaysen says.

"So you what? Thought you'd hitch a ride on the back of your friend who *just* learned how to shift and could probably only make it a few miles? And then, what? Was I going to carry Atta in my owl form?" Pollux glares at Jaysen.

"Well, no, I . . . I guess I didn't think about—" Jaysen stammers.

"Think about someone other than yourself?" Pollux questions.

Jaysen turns and walks down the frozen river, finding some space to be alone.

I glare at Pollux. "You don't have to be so hard on him. He, like me, was thrown into a whole new world. It's not like he understands shifters, and magic. I don't even understand shifters or magic yet. At least I have my own knowledge of my shifting abilities, he has nothing. Give him some fucking grace."

Pollux glares back at me. "Knowledge or not. He shouldn't expect handouts and free rides."

Atta interjects. "That's enough!" she yells, followed by a heavy sigh. "We need to stick together and be protective of one another if we are going to survive this. So quit bickering."

Pollux turns on her. "Oh yeah? When are you going to tell us your little secret?"

Atta's face turns pale. She looks nervous, and I've never seen her nervous before. Come to think of it, I've never seen her anything but confident and happy.

"Pollux, what in all the realms?" I shout.

"I . . . What . . .How do . . . How do you know?" Atta asks.

"Oh, like it isn't obvious? How else do you know everyone's intentions before they even happen?" he questions.

Atta wrings her hands together in front of her. "I didn't think anyone from the Night Realm knew, it isn't a common trait to carry in the Night Realm . . ." she mumbles.

"Yeah, but you're not from the Night Realm, are you?" he asks.

"No, and neither are you," she snaps back. Her tone is accusatory. Like she wasn't sure if she believed him or not, but now she does.

"Can someone please fill me in?" I shout at them.

Pollux grumbles, not taking his eyes off Atta, and says, "Atta here is an intuit. She can feel people's intentions, probably more, but intuits aren't usually honest with the full scope of their abilities . . ."

"That's because we are rare, and often hunted for our abilities, so why would we share with the public? Why should I share with *you*? Where are you really from? Cause you are not from Night," she demands.

Pollux remains quiet.

"Answer her!" I demand.

He turns to me then, locking eyes with me. "Are you really not going to ask more of her?"

"No. I trust her. She has been nothing but a kind and loyal friend since the day I arrived in Night. She's been honest with me every time I asked her a question. She didn't tell anyone about the book, so she obviously trusts me in some way, too. It may be naive and stupid of me to trust her, but I do." I take a deep breath. "You, on the other hand. I feel drawn to you, but you won't acknowledge it. You told me to hide my magic when I arrived, already knowing I had it. You wouldn't tell me why you knew, or why I should trust you. When I showed my magic, not a word was mentioned about me not hiding it, but you began training me for a war I wanted no part of. So, I think you should tell us where you are from."

Pollux's face shifts. Concern etched in every corner. "Are you saying you don't trust me, El?"

"I'm saying you should answer her question. What realm are you from?" I ask again.

He sighs. "To be clear, I trust you."

"To be clear, answer the bloody question and I'll decide if I trust you," I say.

Jaysen walks back over now, concern on his face too.

"What's going on?" he asks.

"Atta is an intuit. I trust her. Pollux won't say where he is from, because it's not Night," I update him.

Jaysen turns to Pollux. "Where in all the gods are you from, man?"

Pollux sighs. "I'm from the Shadow Realm . . ."

My brain feels scrambled for a minute. I've never heard of a Shadow Realm, or I guess I have during the king's proclamation. I don't have any knowledge of it, though.

Wait, that can't be right, because the king said the Shadow Realm is their enemy. That I was leading them to the Summit of Shadows. If Pollux is from there, and also a member of the King's Guard . . .

Atta shouts suddenly, "That's where you're taking us, isn't it?"

Pollux sighs again. "Yes."

Atta questions him, "Why?"

"To keep El safe . . ." he mumbles.

She looks at him, and he looks at her. A solid minute passes, before Atta turns to me. "He's telling the truth, his intentions are to keep you safe."

Pollux groans. "Is this how this is going to be now? How am I supposed to trust her?" He points in Atta's direction.

"We all need to trust each other, or I am moving forward *alone*," I snap. My patience is thin now. I've never had companions or friends, and this thing called trust is already complicated within me, but I know that we need it in order to move forward.

"Does anyone have any other secrets they would like to share before we continue?" I ask.

"Well . . ." Jaysen says, "I left a note for Brock, Selene, and Eos."

We all turn to him. "You what?" Pollux seethes.

"I couldn't just leave them without a word, they are my friends!" he shouts. "They are your friends too!" he shouts at me and Atta, gesturing to us wildly.

"I barely know them," I say.

"Alright, I think that is the signal for us to keep moving. There is nothing we can do now but keep moving forward, otherwise, we are all dead," Atta states. I know she's right, and we should keep moving. I really want to continue talking, and maybe work through some of the hate coursing through everyone currently, but I know with Jaysen's statement just now, we don't have time.

"Let's go for another hour, and then we need to stop and rest. We can set up a camp and take turns keeping guard," Pollux says.

"Okay," Atta replies.

"Do we have stuff to camp? To eat?" I ask.

Pollux and Atta turn to me. "Of course we do," Atta says. "What do you think I have in my bag?"

"You had camping gear packed before knowing we were leaving?" I ask.

She laughs, and gives me a look. Right, intuit. Going to need to get used to that new information. She knew what Pollux was planning. I laugh, because she also probably knew what I was planning. She knew what I kept thinking, and she knew I'd go with him.

"Ah, right," I mumble.

"Let's move," Pollux says.

Everyone gets back on Pegasus and Epona. We continue riding toward the Shadow Realm. A place that I didn't know existed, and I have no idea what to expect.

Chapter Twenty-Two

THE WORLD FEELS HUSHED and slow, and the starlight illuminates our path ahead. We have stopped talking to each other again. The rhythmic sound of the hooves against the ground without distractions threatens to put me to sleep. I try to keep my senses sharp though, forcing myself to notice every tree, every rustle of leaves, and every distant call of an owl or coyote.

The sounds of animals are more terrifying in a world where they could be a shifter. I never had to live with that fear in the Day Realm. I didn't know magic or shifters existed.

My life was much simpler then, my life without magic. It's not hard to see how someone returning to that life would feel insane. Thinking that everything could be a shifter watching you, that anyone could be an intuit, like Atta.

Pegasus moves slowly and carefully. He seems so attuned to the world around him. Like he, too, is taking note of all his surroundings.

The air starts to feel colder, crisper against my skin as we get further north. There's a sense of being untethered from time while riding with nothing but you, the horse, and the stars.

After a few more minutes, the wind begins howling with such ferocity that it drowns out everything else. It is a constant, roaring presence, like standing beneath a crashing waterfall. All our voices vanish into it. Even my own breath seems swallowed by it. It fills my ears, shakes the trees to their roots, and makes the world feel distant. Life is muffled beneath its sheer, relentless force. Every other sound around us, like the pounding of the hooves against the dirt, and the snap of a branch, is erased. All I can hear is the deafening, all-consuming scream of the wind.

Pollux leans in against the wind, as my hair whips wildly across his face like the trees in this storm. The horses keep moving forward on the trail, their hooves thudding over hard ground. All I can feel, though, is *him*—close, urgent, his lips brushing my ear as he starts to speak, just loud enough to pierce the wind's fury. His breath is hot, a jolt of contrast in the cold chaos, and his hand finds my arm for balance. They are firm, instinctive, and possessive. I shiver again, not knowing if it's from the wind or his warm touch.

The wind continues to roar, tearing at our cloaks and reins, but in that moment, it only seems to push us closer together, as if nature itself was forcing our bodies to collide.

Pollux tries to yell over the wind, "We need to stop. The wind is too much!"

I can't tell if he's yelling at me or at Atta. Either way, I agree and nod my head against him.

We find a spot surrounded by trees. I think Pollux hopes they will block out some of the wind. Atta and Pollux work swiftly, trying to put up the tents. The fabric snaps and flails around like a living thing, catching every gust and yanking out of their hands just when I think they've got it pinned. Poles clatter, stakes twist in the loose soil, and the wind steals their curses. It's hard to stand and watch it happen. I yell again and ask if they need any help, but I'm met again with another harsh no.

When they finally get the two tents up, Jaysen comes up and grabs my hand. "Let's get some rest, Elliora. I bet you're tired."

Pollux comes up and physically removes Jaysen's hand from mine.

"She will rest, and so will you . . . in separate tents."

Jaysen stands taller, and puffs out his chest. "I don't think it's your choice, Pollux. I think it's hers. This is her story now." He smiles at me when he says the line at the end, like he wants me to notice he listened.

I'm slightly regretting letting him come along on this journey.

I still don't completely trust him. I'm not sure why he is interested in me. He could've had some of the other girls back at the palace.

I also still can't let go of the fact that he brought up my mom, and never explained more. But to be fair, I haven't asked him about it either.

"Who's taking the first guard shift?" I ask, trying to just get something going. Someone needs to rest right now while we are here, and the tents are finally up.

"I've got it," Atta says. "I couldn't sleep right now even if I wanted to. I'll take the first shift."

"Okay. Atta is on first shift, El and I will take this tent." He gestures to the tent on the left. "Jaysen, take that tent." Pollux states.

"For gods' sake, Pollux! Let Elliora decide!" Jaysen shouts against the wind.

The wind is coming in waves now. One second its brute force is enough to knock me over, the next it's calm and peaceful again. Almost like it's trying to tell me something in a code I don't understand.

Pollux glares at Jaysen. "If something happens, do you have the ability to protect her? The training? Atta and I were members of the King's Guard. Trained to keep royalty safe. What training do you have?"

"I don't need training, Atta is on guard! All of us would wake up if something happened. She doesn't need you to be some knight in shining armor!" he shouts.

"I'm exhausted, and sick of arguing," I mumble. "Let me know what you guys decide . . . I'll be in this tent."

I point over to the tent Pollux had said I would sleep in before.

Jaysen shouts again, "But it's *your* choice! Who do you pick?!"

"Nothing has ever been my choice, except the moment, he said—" I point to Pollux, "do you want to leave? That was my decision for today, and I'm too tired to make another right now. Goodnight, or good day, or whatever." I groan and move into the tent.

There are two sleeping bags in here. I grab one and bundle myself into it.

I breathe in through my nose and out through my mouth, trying to relax.

After a few more minutes, Pollux enters the tent. I already knew he would win that argument. It didn't feel worth hurting Jaysen's feelings when I already knew what the outcome would be.

The tiny tent feels immediately even smaller after Pollux finds his sleeping bag and lies down next to me.

The wind moves the canvas tent rhythmically above us, the noise a soft pulse that muffles the world outside. Inside this small tent, the air is thick, but not with cold, with something heavier. I shift in my sleeping bag, trying to find a position that doesn't have me pressed shoulder-to-shoulder with Pollux in his. It is next to impossible.

"It's still windy." Pollux's voice is low, and his breath is warm where it brushes against my cheek.

I nod. "Yeah, still windy."

He exhales, almost a sigh.

The silence that follows isn't comfortable. It buzzes with everything unsaid between us. The heat from our bodies has nowhere to go. It's trapped in the tight confines of this tent. I can feel every inch of where our bodies touch. The accidental graze of his thigh against mine, and the back of his hand brushing my arm, are absolute agony.

"You're freezing," he murmurs, noticing me shiver.

"I'm fine," I lie.

There is a long pause.

His hand moves slowly, carefully, to my arm, and he wraps his fingers around it. My skin prickles under his touch. But I don't pull away.

"You know," Pollux says, voice rougher now, "we could—share a sleeping bag. For warmth. Just for warmth."

I turn my head to look at him. Our noses nearly brush.

"Okay. Sure, for warmth," I repeat.

Our eyes are locked on each other. His lips part slightly, and I swear I see a tremble of hesitation, or maybe restraint. The moment tilts.

I softly say, "You've been looking at me like that a lot lately."

He doesn't deny it. "You let me."

"Maybe I want you to," I whisper in the dark confines of our tent.

His hand slides slowly up my arm, before curling behind my neck, drawing me in the last inch until our foreheads touch.

"Tell me to stop," he whispers.

I don't.

I've felt this dream before, except this time, he isn't flying off in his owl form.

He kisses me, finally, and it isn't tentative. It is heat and longing, built on every moment of when we haven't said what we are feeling.

The wind roars outside now, but the sound is faded, replaced by the soft sounds of breath and the crinkle of our sleeping bags shifting.

He pulls me closer, his hand slipping down to the small of my back, and I let myself melt into the weight of him, into the tension that has finally snapped.

Outside, the wind rages. Inside, it is something else entirely.

He pulls away abruptly. "I'm sorry. I— we should get some rest." He rolls over, moving his back to me. My swollen lips ache for more. My heart pounds in my chest.

I shift uncomfortably at the heat between my legs. The need that sits there wanting more.

I roll over, too.

"I'm not sorry," I whisper into the side of the tent.

I lay there realizing, it wasn't another dream. This time it was better than a dream, the best kiss I've ever had, yet he immediately regretted it.

I stare at the side of the tent. Tears prickle behind my eyes as I fall asleep.

I wake up abruptly, and Atta is sitting in the sleeping bag Pollux was in, reading a book. "Well, hello sunshine, ready to keep moving? I think the boys are." She smiles at me.

I smile at her. "Atta, did you sleep at all?" I ask.

"Nope. Not really. I may have gotten a few minutes, but I'll be honest, your intentions are practically yelling at me. It's impossible to drown them out." She rubs at her temples. "No worries though, I'm used to functioning on very little sleep." She winks at me.

"My intentions are . . .yelling at you?" I whisper.

"Oh yeah, just tell him how you feel already. Please, for both of our sakes." She starts rolling up the sleeping bag.

"Who?" I ask.

"Honestly, now that you mention it, both of them." She laughs.

I listen outside the tent. I no longer hear the wind howling, and the tent isn't moving steadily like it was when I fell asleep last night.

I roll over and look at Atta. "So you're an intuit?" I whisper. I don't know why I whisper it, we all know now. It just still feels like some kind of secret.

She sighs. "Yeah, I hope you aren't mad. There were a million times I wanted to tell you, I just couldn't."

"Because of the king? Or because you didn't want me to know?" I ask.

Atta grimaces. "It sounds bad, but both? I've never told *anyone*, the closest I've ever come to telling someone was you. But when you've had a past like mine, you don't really want to share that information with anyone . . ."

I nod my head. I don't understand her past, but I do understand feeling like you need to hide part of yourself. How many times did I dream of stars in Swaylin? I never told a soul after the reaction my mother had when I confided in her. I believe she wanted to tell me, but was scared. It's hard to trust someone.

"You don't need to worry Atta, I understand." I smile at her, and I know she knows where my head is at, or at least what my intentions are.

It's a weird feeling to get used to, but it's also somewhat comforting. To know that she does trust me, because she knows I don't intend to hurt her in any way, ever.

"Sooooo, since you're an intuit, Jaysen? I get the feeling there is something off about him? I can't bring myself to . . ." I lower my voice, "fully trust him."

She wrinkles her nose. "I don't fully trust him, someone has taught him to put up a wall in his mind, something that I sometimes *wish* they would've taught you." She laughs, and then continues, "He's not very good at it, though, his intentions sneak through occasionally but they are broken. They are normally about you: keeping you safe, making sure you're healthy. I'll be honest, though, I can only see intentions. It's not like I can read his mind. I've never felt a *bad* intention from him, but that doesn't mean they aren't locked away somewhere in there."

"Who could teach him how to do something like that? How to build a wall?" I question.

Atta shrugs. "There are probably a few people who know how to do it in the Night Realm, but why would they teach *him?* When Jaysen first arrived his intention was to find 'the one'. I assumed it was the one from the prophecy, because that was all I got from him. But honestly, isn't that what *everyone* in the Night Realm was looking for? I didn't think much of it at the time. Until . . . well, you. Because why did he know about the prophecy? You didn't know anything of the prophecy before arriving here right? So, why did he?"

It's odd to think about. Why *does* Jaysen worry so much about me, when he only just met me on our way here? I assumed it was an alliance of sorts, but now I'm not sure. But also, why did Jaysen know there was someone to be found here?

"I'm also not the best intuit, Ellie. I've never told anyone, and my parents died before I developed my abilities, so no one has ever taught me. I've just figured it out as I went. He could have a bad intention, but he seems . . . dumb," she whispers.

"I don't know, Atta. I wish I knew. He's never given me reason to suspect he's up to something *bad*. He just seems like he has something he isn't saying," I whisper.

"Yeah, I don't know. I wish I knew more, but he's getting better and better at building his wall." She sighs. "I wonder why someone taught him that in the first place? Do you think someone in Night suspected there was an intuit? What if it was Pollux?"

I laugh. "It wasn't Pollux, he hates Jaysen and would never teach him anything."

She laughs too. "You're right, that was silly. I just didn't think anyone was on to me, and obviously Pollux was. I wonder who else was."

"Well, Atta, no matter what, the four of us are in this together now. If you do sense something off, tell me. Otherwise, I think we just need to trust each other for now. At least, until we make it somewhere safe. Then we can re-evaluate," I state.

"Okay, Ellie. I'll do my best." She salutes me, and then laughs.

I throw my pillow at her.

"I guess I should go help Pollux now." She stands.

I sit up and grab my bag, as Atta gets up and exits the tent. I rummage through my things, and change my pants. I don't know if I have enough clothes for this journey, so I'm going to keep the shirt I have on, for now.

As I dig through my bag, the ring King Canis gave me falls to the ground. I forgot I packed it the night we left. I thought we might need it for money at some point.

I turn it over in my hand. It's beautiful but represents a million things I'm unsure about. Should I have fled before I figured it out? I'm still not sure, but I already made the decision and I need to make the best of it now.

I slip the ring on my finger. I think it's safer on me than it is loose in an old canvas bag.

I quickly pack up everything else, and exit the tent.

Jaysen brings me a tiny bit of food. "Good morning Elliora, here is some food."

"Thanks." I smile at him and I glance around. The other tent is already gone, packed up with the horses. Pollux and Atta have already started breaking down the tent I was just in.

I guess they think we really need to get moving, before someone catches up to us.

"Are we worried at all about the king using his dragon form to catch us?" I ask Atta and Pollux.

They exchange a look.

"Not particularly, he doesn't have the best flying abilities in his form. He can burn down a city, but flight has always been hard for him," Atta says.

Pollux sighs. "We still need to keep moving, there are plenty of other fast shifters on the King's Guard and I'm sure they are on the hunt. Especially after Jaysen left a damned note."

"Let's just go, I'm not ready for another fight." I sigh, and we make our way to the horses.

I walk up to Pegasus and pet him gently on the nose. I whisper positive affirmations to him and tell him that he's a good boy.

He huffs at me, and I laugh.

It's the first time I laugh without effort. I've always loved animals, but the Night Realm has brought out a new appreciation for them.

Pollux walks up next to me and holds out his hand to help me up onto Pegasus. I place my hand in his, and look down at my feet. Suddenly, Pollux is gripping my hand so tightly, the pressure almost makes me scream. I turn to look at him.

His eyes blaze with fury. "El, what the fuck is on your hand?" he seethes.

Chapter Twenty-Three

My chest tightens, and I try to breathe normally. His grip on my hand threatens to break a bone. I try to smile, but fail miserably.

"Oh," I say, my voice too soft. I clear my throat. "I just thought I should bring it along, in case we needed to exchange it for monetary value."

"But, why are you wearing it?" His grip lightens as he speaks.

"I just . . . thought I should put it on so it wasn't loose in my bag. I didn't want to lose it," I mumble.

At this point, Jaysen and Atta are yelling at us, asking what in the gods is taking us so long.

I look at Pollux; the tension slowly fades from his face. He lets go of my hand completely.

"Sorry . . . I . . . I don't know what came over me. Let's head out," he smiles, and reaches his hand out to help me up again.

Pollux confuses me in every possible way. One moment he is all warmth and closeness, a flame flickering toward me. The next, he vanishes behind a wall of ice, and I'm left questioning whether the fire has ever been real.

"Maybe I should shift? I'm feeling uncomfortable and it might be nice to just walk for a while?" I whisper.

"Jaysen doesn't know you can shift into anything other than a dragon. I think you should keep it that way for at least a little bit longer," he says. "We need to make sure we can trust him."

As if he knew we were speaking of him, Jaysen shouts, "What are we waiting for?"

I look over at Jaysen. Impatience written all over his face.

I can't decide if Jaysen is untrustworthy or just dumb. Learning that he left some kind of note back at the Night Realm Palace makes me think he's just a dumb boy. A dumb boy who hasn't quite figured out how to become a man.

He gets defensive easily, and avoids any hard conversations. His sense of entitlement and refusal to accept adult responsibilities are key signs that he hasn't quite matured into a dependable, self-aware individual yet.

So I try to give him the benefit of the doubt.

I look back at Pollux, who has masked his face in a sense of calm once again. He holds out his hand to help me up onto Pegasus.

I sigh. He's right, though. I shouldn't show Jaysen all my secrets just yet.

I grab his hand and lift myself up onto Pegasus.

Two hours later, we are still riding north in silence.

It seems we have returned to the fear of someone hearing us if we speak, or maybe it's just that no one wants to.

I tell myself it's the former. I'm obviously completely unfamiliar with the area, so I have no idea if people inhabit these areas.

Pollux has one hand resting lightly around my waist, the sway and rhythm of Pegasus bringing us closer together.

I listen to the various sounds of the forest: a bird singing, the creak of saddle leather, the rhythm of the hooves. I turn my head slightly to glance at Atta and Jaysen. They look much less comfortable on a horse together than we are. I sneak a glance up at Pollux; his sharp jawline points straight ahead. Yet, there is the tiniest tilt upward at the corner of his mouth. He looks down at me, smiles, and then looks back at the trail ahead.

It's rare, the moments he smiles, but they are my favorite moments.

My body starts to grow tired. I lean back slightly as Pegasus climbs a hill. I can feel the rise and fall of Pollux's breath.

Even though I'm leaning back into him slightly, it's deliberate. I'm making a soft but unmistakable gesture of trust and closeness.

I feel slightly guilty for implying I don't trust him yesterday. I obviously wouldn't have come on this journey if I didn't. However, the hot and cold of emotions with him makes it hard to fully trust him if I'm being honest.

I know he feels this pull, this magnetic feeling I have toward him. I can tell sometimes in small gestures, that he feels it too, but he pulls back. He puts up walls, and that's why I can't trust him completely. If he would just show me his feelings, and let me in, I think I could give him my heart.

My back meets his chest, and my shoulders brush back against him. I rest my head lightly against him, and tilt it up just enough in hopes he can hear my wordless cue: *I'm comfortable with you, I want to be close.*

For a second, the world narrows and the tension between us escalates. It's gentle, electric, and waiting. Pollux shifts slightly in response, pulling me closer to him. He's breathing a little deeper, and letting the moment stretch between us.

It's not loud or obvious, but it means something.

As we keep moving forward, all I can feel is him, the warmth of this moment, and the quiet promise that maybe—just maybe—we are moving toward something more.

And I *really* hope we are.

We eventually stop to take another break. Time is starting to feel like an illusion. I have no idea what time of day it is, or what meal I should be eating by now, but my stomach grumbles, so I know I'm missing something.

We all hop off the horses and stretch. I wander off with Atta to relieve ourselves amongst the trees, because apparently, I can't even have a minute to myself for that anymore.

The wind has picked up again. It seems like it always does when something bad is coming.

I turn to Atta. "Can we just stay here another minute? I just need one more second away from them."

"Sure." Atta plops down and lays herself in the grass.

I decide to lay down next to her.

I look up at the stars and find my peace once again.

It's crazy to think that a few months ago I had never seen a star, and now I couldn't imagine my life without them. I don't know how I'll ever live without the peace and sense of calm they bring me.

I press my back into the cold grass, my hands are shaking from the tension curled like a snake inside me. I can feel it building, the quiet thrum of instincts trying to take the wheel. My body is chanting *shift. You need to shift. Now.*

Atta glances over at me. "You good?" she asks.

I wonder if she can hear it. Can she hear the intentions of the beast inside me? Roaring to be let free?

I grind my teeth together, and push the sensation back down. "Yep, all good." I smile.

She smiles, and looks back up at the stars.

The world around me doesn't care that I'm about to lose control. Life continues to go on around me.

I try to focus on the stars again, when I see it. The moon. It is high in the sky, mocking me, practically demanding I shift. I take a deep breath. It's such a beautiful thing, I wish the first time I saw it was under different circumstances. I wish I was seeing it while I didn't have a war raging inside of me.

I stare at it for another minute, following its curve with my eyes while focusing on my breathing. It doesn't bring me a sense of calm the way the stars do, in fact, I think it makes my anxiety heighten.

"Let's get back to them before they worry." I jump up, and reach down, giving Atta my hand. As she grabs it, I start to lift her up, when another wave hits me. It's stronger this time. My knees buckle. I fall forward, catching myself with trembling hands.

Atta shouts, "Whoa, girl, are you okay?"

"Not yet," I whisper. "Not here," I tell myself.

Pollux and Jaysen come running over.

"What is going on? Elliora, are you okay?" Jaysen asks.

I breathe deep, and finally, there is silence within me.

I stand up. "Yeah, sorry, I'm okay. I think I just need a snack or something."

Everyone glances at me warily.

"I promise I'm good, let's just keep going!" I smile, and make my way back to the horses. I focus on putting one foot in front of the other, and walking calmly so none of them worry.

Everyone hesitantly makes their way back to the horses with me. I take one last stretch before climbing up onto Pegasus. Atta and Jaysen climb up onto Epona. Pollux looks me up and down another time. "Are you sure you're okay?" he asks.

"Yep! Let's keep going." I smile.

Pollux swings up onto Pegasus behind me in one fluid motion. He makes it look so easy. Pegasus shifts slightly, and Pollux puts his one hand around my waist again.

We continue north.

We finally stop for rest hours later.

Everyone seems disappointed that we didn't make it farther today, but the horses are tired, and so are we. We need to stop for all of our health and safety.

The wind is roaring once again. Atta makes a comment about how unusual all of the wind has been. I really wouldn't know, as I've never been to this area before.

"Is it unusual?" I ask Pollux. I figure he's the only one who would truly know.

"It is . . . odd, but stranger things have happened." He shrugs.

Pollux and Atta fight against the breeze again to get the tents up. I ask Jaysen to help me feed the horses since I know they won't let me help with the tents.

Once the horses are fed, I gently pet Pegasus. I look up at Jaysen, who is already looking at me.

"You doing okay?" he asks. "I'm worried about you."

I smile. "That's so sweet, but there is nothing to worry about." I pause, thinking over the question I've been dying to ask him. "Jaysen, can I ask you something?"

"Sure, Elliora! You can always ask me anything." He grins at me, and moves a couple of steps closer.

"Why did you come? Like, when you saw us leaving the palace that night? Why did you come with us? You had friends at the castle. Close enough friends that you left a note." I sigh. "I know I kind of did too, but I was going to be forced to marry, what was your reason?"

He thinks for a second. "I know it probably isn't the answer you want but, I don't really know. It just felt right, there was some kind of voice inside me that said this is your chance, take it!" He sighs. "I wish I had something more for you than that. I like you, Elliora, I have since we met on the ship, and for whatever reason, I think I'd follow you to the ends of this world."

He sighs. "I smile a lot, and stay positive. I wasn't always that way, though. I've just learned that if I'm not trusting my gut and staying positive, I can get myself into trouble."

"What kind of trouble?" I ask.

Atta shouts, "Tents and dinner are ready. Come on, let's eat!"

Jaysen smiles. "I guess that's a story for another day."

Chapter Twenty-Four

AFTER FINALLY BATHING IN a nearby creek, the four of us sit around a fire that Atta made and eat a small amount of food. I can feel life coming back into me after the simple act of cleaning myself, and filling my stomach with a small snack of food.

Pollux tells us the unfortunate news that we only have one more day's worth of food left, since he didn't pack enough for Jaysen *and* Atta originally. I immediately feel defeated again.

"I really only packed enough for El and I if I'm being honest. I brought extra, but not enough for four. It should be fine, though, we should make it across the border tomorrow. If I'm rationing you at all, though, that's why," Pollux says.

"Really? We will get there tomorrow?" I'm nervous and excited. "Tell me something about this . . . Shadow Realm. I don't know anything, and neither does Jaysen."

It still sounds odd to me, all I've ever known is Day and Night. I guess I imagined other lands might exist, but never truly thought about it for long enough.

Pollux smiles. "El, you're going to love it."

Atta turns her head swiftly and glares at Pollux. "What was that?"

Pollux looks at her confused. "What was what?"

Atta stands up, pointing at him. "That intention! When you told her she'd love it, you're hiding something!"

Pollux stands up too. "It's not what you think, Atta, calm down."

"I will not calm down, this girl is my family now. Somehow she weaseled her way into my heart and she is the only person I have cared about since . . ." Her voice cracks.

"You know what? Let's all get some rest. We can talk in the morning on horseback. Tensions seem high, and everyone is exhausted," I say. I stand too, and Jaysen follows suit.

"Can I trust you tonight?" Atta asks Pollux.

I know what she is doing. She's trying to read his intentions for the night, to see if we are safe to leave this conversation for tomorrow. It's smart, and I don't blame her.

Pollux locks eyes with Atta. "Atta, I would never, and I mean ever, hurt El on purpose. All I want is to protect her and get her to safety. That's the whole reason we left Night Realm. She couldn't marry that . . . that . . . monster."

Atta sighs. "I know, sorry, I just needed to know. You're hiding something, though."

"It's fine, It's nothing that matters Atta," Pollux says, "and I would be more worried if you didn't care."

"I think at this point, we can all just agree that we care about one another." I smile.

Pollux grunts, "Nope, I don't care about Jaysen. At all. If something happens, I will make you use him as your human shield."

"Pollux!" I shout.

Jaysen laughs. "It's fine, Elliora, that feeling goes both ways."

Pollux continues to glare at Jaysen.

"Okay, well as fun as it is to watch you guys have a staring contest, I'm going to rest now." I sigh.

Atta smiles at me. "I'll take the first watch again."

Pollux grunts. "Atta, you sure? I don't mind."

Atta grins. "Based on the atmosphere right now. I think you and Ellie need a second to . . . talk"

Jaysen stomps his foot and crosses his arms. "What about me! I need to talk to Elliora too."

The way he throws a tantrum reminds me of the smaller kids back home in Swaylin. It seems Jaysen still throws a tantrum when things don't go his way.

"I'm not talking with anyone. I'm resting. It sounds like we need to make it there tomorrow since our food is running low. Right?" I gesture to Pollux.

"Right," Pollux says.

"Okay, and we still have a bit of a journey ahead, correct?" I ask him again.

"That's correct," he states.

"Great, then I will be resting, and I think whoever isn't currently on watch should do the same." I turn and make my way toward the tents.

The tents are much more spread out tonight due to the terrain and the wind. As I get to the tent I will be sleeping in, I turn around. The three of them are all still standing around the fire, whispering, probably about me.

Tears prickle behind my eyes. I've never felt close to anyone. My grandfather was the closest thing I ever had, but in comparison to the love I feel now for these three, I don't even know if my grandfather loved me all those years.

Maybe he just felt bad for me, and tried to make my time with them less miserable. There was always an element of fear behind his eyes when he would talk to me.

I guess he knew something I didn't.

These three, though, they don't have that.

They don't have the glossy look of fear or the angry look of hatred.

I don't know if any of them will ever say it out loud, but I can feel it, in the small things they do and the quiet moments. They care about me, in their own ways, and they show it. Somehow, they've come to feel like family. Not the kind I knew growing up, but the kind I used to imagine when I saw other kids with their families laughing, feeling safe, and *belonging*.

It's not perfect, and it's not always spoken, but it's real. And that's enough for me.

I shout to them, "Hey!" They all turn and look at me. "This may be weird, but I just want you all to know I care about you. Thanks for being with me on this journey."

I turn, because I can't handle the thought of their reactions.

I climb into the tent, and strip down to fewer clothes to be comfortable in my sleeping bag.

I gaze up at the swaying tent roof as the wind howls outside, grateful I spoke my truth. Tomorrow is never certain, and I needed them to know I care.

I hear Pollux come into the tent a few minutes later, and I sit up.

His gold eyes glow with an eerie brilliance, catching and reflecting even the faintest light within the tent. The golden hue is intense, like molten amber or polished brass, shining against the darkness of the tent. They are both beautiful and haunting, he looks like a silent predator watching from the shadows, his eyes piercing with a luminous stare that feels otherworldly.

He breaks off the heated gaze and makes his way to the side of his sleeping bag, taking his weapons, cloak, boots, and jacket off. I roll over. I'm not sure how much more he is going to take off before getting in his sleeping bag, but I can't bear to watch.

It's a quiet kind of chaos.

We are lying side by side in the dark, and we are so close I can hear his breath shift with every movement. I shouldn't want him; maybe he's taken, or maybe there's history. He could have a friendship, or something. I don't know, we haven't ever talked about it. But I know I wasn't imagining the desire in his heated glances, and I definitely didn't imagine that very real kiss. I wish I could get a read on him.

Here, though, in this small shared space, all those reasons feel somewhat abstract. They feel like rules written for a different reality. Our bodies aren't touching, but my awareness of him fills the air between us like static.

I roll over and lay on my back, my eyes focused on the dark ceiling. I think to myself, *don't roll over, don't look, don't want.*

But I do, and the worst part is I'm pretty sure he does too.

That's the tension, the wanting and waiting, in the silence of this zipped-up world. I'm pretending that the nearness doesn't mean everything.

"El . . ." Pollux whispers.

I should pretend I'm asleep. He regretted kissing me last night, and I need to just ignore him.

I ignore my gut, though, and roll over to look at him anyway. "Yeah?"

"I . . ." he whispers, and then sighs.

The silence that fills the tent is unbearable.

"I wasn't going to say anything, I really wasn't. I had a whole plan of keeping this to myself until it faded or disappeared or until I convinced myself this wasn't real. But the truth is, it *is* real. It's been real for a while now. I think about you at the most inconvenient times. I look for you in a room before I even realize I'm doing it. When something good happens, you're the first person I want to tell. When everything falls apart, I want to fall apart with you. And I know I shouldn't be saying this, because I shouldn't want this. I can't want this. It's honestly going to ruin everything—but I need you to know." His voice cracks and he takes a deep breath.

"Pollux, I . . ." I whisper in the dark tent.

"El, I don't know what you're supposed to do with that, and I'm not expecting anything. I just, I can't keep carrying it around like it's not breaking me a little more every day," he whispers.

I scoot my sleeping bag closer to him and grab his face with both my hands.

"Pollux, I feel the same way. From the moment I first saw you, something shifted in me, something I still don't fully understand. I've never really cared for anyone before... Honestly, I've never even cared about myself. But now that you're in my life, I can't imagine a world without you. Words fail me, but what I feel for you is real, more real than anything I've ever known."

And then I kiss him.

Chapter Twenty-Five

As HEARTFELT AS OUR speeches were, this kiss is anything but graceful. It's awkward and clumsy as we both try to untangle ourselves from our sleeping bags, our hands fumbling, lips missing, and laughter slipping out when we can't quite find our rhythm. But somehow, that makes it even more perfect.

When we are finally out of our sleeping bags, Pollux glides his hands up into my hair and tilts my head up to face him. I smile.

Our lips meet together a little too aggressively. Our teeth hit together, and we quietly laugh.

Without saying, we are both trying to be quiet, unsure of what Jaysen and Atta can hear outside the tent.

And then he kisses me again, and again. Slower and softer this time, both of us starting to notice what the other responds to.

One second I'm Elliora, a girl who didn't care if she even lived to see tomorrow, and the next I'm El, the girl who is completely and irrevocably caught up in a passionate kiss with Pollux.

He moves away. "If we act on this, it could be the end of both of us, but I just can't deny it anymore."

"Pollux, I don't care, I need this," I whisper.

"But El, I . . ."

He doesn't finish the sentence, because I sweep my tongue up the side of his neck. "Don't stop," I mumble against his neck, before nipping at his ear lobe.

It feels like my body, heart, and soul are all waking up at once. It feels as though I've been asleep for years without knowing it. There's no thought of tomorrow, no fear of what comes next. Just this moment, right here, with a man I never expected... but now I can't imagine living without him.

This kiss means something, undeniably so. I know it does for him too, because he doesn't rush it. He lingers, like he wants to memorize every second of it.

I pull apart, and look into Pollux's glowing golden eyes. I run my hand up his stubble along his jaw. His eyes are intense and determined. Neither of us speak out loud. But a conversation happens between us anyway.

I sit up and grab the hem of my shirt, and lift it up over my head, taking my bra off quickly behind it.

I can visibly see Pollux swallow.

I sit there shirtless, and Pollux sits up and grabs my face. "You're gorgeous, El," he whispers.

I reach down to the hem of his shirt, searching his eyes, questioning. He nods, and I lift his shirt up over his head.

I take a minute to admire the black ink that lines most of his body. I've spent every day since the first day I saw him trying to envision what these lines would look like.

The lines swirl like shadows across his muscular frame.

I throw the shirt to the side, and trace every line on his abdomen, every muscle, and every scar. He's stunning. He looks like he was sculpted by the gods, and I can't imagine what he sees in a girl like me.

I look up at him, and his eyes blaze.

"I said, you are gorgeous, El. I'm going to make whatever you're thinking completely disappear." He pushes me back onto the top of my sleeping bag, and grabs the waist of my pants, sliding them down completely.

He takes his time, taking off my socks and then moving his way up my leg with kisses. Pressing each kiss tenderly into my skin, when he finally reaches the inside of my thigh, I gasp.

"No more thoughts, El. Just pleasure," and then he puts his mouth on me. In a way no one has before, and his tongue dives in, making me see stars *inside* the tent.

He reaches one hand up and palms my breast, before putting my nipple between his fingers and teasing. His tongue continues to move inside me, eventually finding my clit.

I feel like I could combust right here and now. The wild tension I felt ten minutes earlier is now pulled tight and about to explode in my core. My toes curl into the sleeping bag at the sensation.

I'm breathless, as I try to find the words. "Pollux, I feel . . . I feel like . . ." I whisper.

Pollux pulls his face out from between my thighs. "Shh, El. I want to give you all the pleasure, but you have to be quiet."

He kisses my thigh again, and then swirls one finger over the place he just kissed. He pulls himself up so he is face-to-face with me while continuing to swirl his finger so close to my entrance. It's teasing, and I can't focus on anything other than the feeling of wanting *more*.

"Do you feel like you're going to come, El?" he asks as he sinks two fingers into me.

"I . . ." I moan. I can't form any thoughts.

He moves his head down and takes my nipple in his mouth, swirling his tongue around it, while his fingers twist inside me.

"Oh, Pollux," I moan again.

He pulls his mouth off my nipple.

"Shhh, El." He smirks up at me. "I don't want anyone to enjoy the sounds you make, no one but *me*."

My legs shake at his words, the pressure building inside of me. His fingers thrust harder now, and he presses his thumb down on my clit, almost holding me in place.

I moan quietly, and gently grind myself into his fingers, needing more pressure.

Pollux whispers, "That's it, El, ride my fingers."

His voice is husky and sensual. My body tingles at his words. I move a little more, finding that perfect amount of pressure.

He pauses his movement, and I whimper.

"Tell me how you want it, El? With my tongue or my fingers?" he whispers in my ear.

I can't think, and I don't know what to say. Suddenly, he grabs my nipple and twists it hard. I cry out.

"Tongue," I gasp.

He pulls both fingers out, and I cry out again, at the release of pressure, instantly missing him and needing more.

He dives down and kisses both my thighs, before putting my legs up over his shoulders.

"I'm all yours, El," he whispers before grabbing my ass, lifting me up and greedily taking me in his mouth.

I lift my arm up to cover my mouth, biting down on my skin to keep from screaming at the pleasure. It's too much, it feels too good.

My legs shake on his shoulders, as the pressure inside me builds. Just as Pollux, drives into my clit one final time, and the world crumbles around me.

I close my eyes and moan into my arm.

I see stars. I pull my arm down and moan as quietly as I can, "Pollux!"

He doesn't let up, though. He continues to drive his tongue into me as I ride the waves, until I melt in his hands.

I'm completely delirious by the time Pollux pushes up onto his knees and slides my legs down and apart.

His pants are still on, but I can see the massive bulge threatening to rip his pants apart. The sparkle in his golden eyes as he looks down at me like I'm his last meal.

I still have a hard time processing that he isn't secretly one of the more ferocious shifters. A lion, or a tiger, or even a dragon himself. When he does things like this, it just feels like he has more in him than I'd expect from an owl.

I smile up at him.

"You ready for another, El?" He smiles back.

"Oh, I don't know," I whisper.

"I do." He pulls his pants down and then stands up, hunched over in the tent. He's too tall for it. He finishes pulling his pants off completely, and climbs back down over me, kissing me roughly on the mouth.

"Come on, El, give me one more." He smiles, and I melt into putty.

I'd give this man anything he wants right now. I nod my head.

He smiles, and then I finally look down. His enormous cock is staring me down. I gulp, because I'm a little nervous.

"You've got it, El," he whispers, and then plunges his cock into me. I pull my arm up again and cover my mouth to hold back the scream that threatens to send Jaysen and Atta running in here at full speed.

"Shhhh, El," he whispers with a chuckle as he begins to rock inside me.

He leans over and presses a kiss against my lips. "I can't wait to fill this sweet pussy with my cum and mark you as *mine*," he whispers.

Inch by delicious inch, he pushes his way inside me.

He fills every bit of space, like I was made to fit him.

He grips my thighs, lifting my legs up as he draws out and pushes back in.

He rocks his hips, and his eyes search mine as I wrap my legs around him.

My legs are around his waist, and my arms are around his neck. He kisses my neck and whispers in my ear, "El, you take me so well," before biting at my earlobe.

He takes a moment to kiss down my neck. He grabs both my hands and pins them up above my head. He moves back into me and continues with a slow, yet exhilarating pace, building pressure within me again. I want to shout with pleasure, but hold back.

We kiss again, and my skin is scorching hot against him. With the sensation of every touch, and every slide in, I feel tears prickle behind my eyes.

"It's too much," I whisper to him, and I don't mean the pressure.

His hips hit me harder. "I've got you, El. You can take it."

I moan. It's too good. I can't even make sense of the pleasure coursing through my body.

With every thrust, I cry out. My toes curl, and the pressure turns into those little white stars in the corner of my vision.

"Pollux, I . . ." I whisper.

"Oh gods, yes, El." He thrusts faster and harder. Putting all the pressure against my clit. My knees buckle around him, and I melt as I completely combust once again.

It's somehow even better the second time.

I cry out, and I don't even know what I'm saying. It's just a wordless noise. Pollux finds his release then, cock twitching and spasming inside me. The waves of pleasure wash over us both.

He falls against me, both of us breathing heavily, and I can feel his smile against my skin.

He kisses me again. "I am positive I could watch you come over and over, for another two million years, and it would never get old."

I laugh. "Oh yeah, and how do I look now?"

I imagine the sweaty, flushed mess that I currently am. Especially after a couple days on horseback.

He smiles and presses a tender kiss to my lips. "You look like you're mine."

Chapter Twenty-Six

I WAKE THE NEXT morning, feeling ready to take on whatever comes our way. After a night of pleasure, I slept better than I have in a while, even sleeping on the floor of a forest. I roll over to say good morning to Pollux, but Atta sits there reading a book.

I groan. "Please tell me you actually slept last night."

"Yep, I did!" She smiles. "Best I've slept in a while now that some of your intentions are quiet and not yelling at me anymore."

She winks at me.

"Atta!" I yell at her, and look around for something to throw at her.

She laughs. "Well, it's true. Plus, I won't tell anyone."

"Ugh!" I shout.

She smiles. "Do you think this is what it feels like?"

"What?" I ask her.

"To have a family? A sister?" Her face is no longer smiling. She looks at me with concern. Like she is worried I won't say what she is hoping I'll say.

Which is funny, because I'm pretty sure she already knows how I feel.

"I do know how you feel, but sometimes a feeling isn't real until it's said out loud. I learned that the hard way . . ."

Leaving me wanting to ask more, but I don't.

"Yeah, Atta, I think this is what it feels like." My eyes water as I say it.

I've come so far since I left Swaylin.

Pollux yells outside the tent, "Atta, you guys almost ready? We need to get moving."

"Yep!" Atta says while hopping up. "Be right out!" she shouts back.

She turns to me. "Thanks, Ellie. Now get ready. I'll be outside the tent waiting for you." She smiles, and then heads out the open flap of the tent.

I'm ready, I've got friends now, though they feel more like family. I have people who care about me, and I care about them. I'm confident we can handle whatever comes our way.

About thirty minutes later, we are on horseback heading north again. I hope this is the last day we have to do this. I'm completely miserable riding horseback. It doesn't help that my whole body now aches to shift. It's begging me.

My time on a ship was eye-opening and fun, but my time on a horse has been quite the opposite. Of course, I do love Pegasus, but I would be perfectly fine if I never had to ride him again. I just want to pet him, and give him treats.

Pollux is relaxed at my back. Jaysen and Atta seem more relaxed with each other now, too. There is a quiet comfort as we stroll through the forest now. Everyone is still on high alert with our surroundings, but not with each other.

"I think I used to dream about you, or some version of you, before I even came to the Night Realm," I whisper quietly to Pollux.

It's something I've wanted to tell him for a while now.

I feel his body tense behind me.

"Ah, well . . . uh . . . what do you mean?" he quietly mumbles.

"I don't know. I used to have these vivid dreams as a child, there was an owl. I knew in my soul, though, that the owl was a person. I can't really explain it, or put it into words. I have hundreds of drawings, and words written in a journal. The owl in my dreams always spoke this gibberish." I laugh. "I don't know. It might have all been nonsense, but I think my heart knew I was looking for an owl someday."

I turn slightly to smile up at him.

He isn't smiling, though.

"What color was the owl?" he whispers against my ear.

"The same color as you in your owl form, but it had these haunting blue-gray eyes . . ."

Pollux's grip on the reins tightens.

"We should stop talking, we are getting close to the mists," he says.

I frown. "Did I say something to upset you? I thought it would be cute to tell you, owls have always been on my mind."

"It's fine, El. Let's just be quiet, though, we are close," he states, eyes on the trail ahead.

"Okay." My heart sinks.

I have this strange feeling that I said something wrong.

About two hours later, we begin descending the slope of a hill. The horses stumble under the strain, and exhaustion clings to all of us like a second skin. Jaysen has voiced his discomfort more than once today, groaning about his aching limbs. As for me, even the simple act of staying upright feels like a battle I'm slowly losing.

As we descend to the bottom, an immense wall of mist rises before us. It's both awe-inspiring and deeply unsettling. It appears almost solid, like a barrier carved from smoke, yet it's clearly just fog. Still, there's something about it that feels alive, as if it's watching, and waiting for us.

"What in all the realms is that?" I whisper.

"*That* is The Great Divide," Atta says with a hint of wonder.

Jaysen looks like he might cry at the sight. "Are we going *through* that?" His voice shakes.

"Yes," Pollux and Atta say in unison.

I shiver. The wind is picking up again, whether urging me on or telling me to turn back, I don't know. But there is no turning back now, so I pull my coat tighter around me.

Pollux rubs a hand up my left arm, trying to warm me.

"Well," Atta says. "What's the plan, Captain?" She smirks at Pollux.

He sighs. "I've made the crossing before. We need to stay close and stay together. It'll take about twenty minutes to make it through completely."

Atta looks at Pollux as if he has grown horns. "One, why in the gods have you made this crossing before? What are you hiding? And two, why would we go to another king? Don't you have a better plan than that?"

"That's my plan, Atta. You asked, there it is." They stare at each other, both with a sense of pride and protective-ness.

"Okay, well, Atta. Any intuition that Pollux is trying to hurt us?" I ask her.

"El, don't you trust me by now?" Pollux asks.

I keep staring at Atta.

"No," Atta mumbles.

"Great, then we stick with his plan," I state.

"Fine." Atta groans.

Pollux rolls his eyes. "Great, well, I say we tie the horse together. It's hard to see in the mists, and it'll make sure we don't get separated."

"Fine," Atta grumbles, leaping off her horse. She walks over as Pollux gets off ours.

"Seems like a good time to take a quick break." I jump off Pegasus, and walk very slowly to the edge of the mists. I place a hand on it, and my hand falls through. I'm not sure what I expected, but the cold mist tingles my skin.

Jaysen walks up, shivering.

"I'm so uncomfortable, Elliora. I don't know if I can do this," he whispers.

I turn to look at him, his puppy dog eyes staring at me, now slightly glossed over. His tan skin is starting to pale from our time here in The Night Realm.

I grab his hand and swirl my thumb over the top of his hand, providing a sense of comfort.

"You can do this, Jaysen. You're one of the bravest peo-ple I know," I whisper.

He nods.

"I can do this for you." He smiles at me.

Suddenly, Atta shouts, "Someone is coming!" right as a man pops out of the mists.

Atta and Pollux have their weapons drawn and at his neck in seconds.

His hands are up in the air.

Chapter Twenty-Seven

THE MAN BEFORE ME appears older, perhaps around my grandfather's age. Strands of gray thread through his hair, and a rough stubble shadows his jawline. His bright blue eyes are warm and inviting, yet they stand in sharp contrast to the deep frown etched across his face.

"Leon!" Pollux shouts, dropping his sword to his side, and sheathing it.

Pollux shakes Leon's hand.

Leon still wears a frown. "Good morrow, Pollux."

"You are right on time." Pollux grins. "I didn't know if you'd be here since we were slightly delayed in our journey . . . multiple times."

"I've been camping on the other side of the Great Divide for days, waiting. Didn't want you to have to cross without me," he says.

Atta and I share a glance. There is something off about this guy. He looks nice, but . . . I'm not sure. I can't quite place it.

I push the feeling down, because I haven't been around enough people in my lifetime to be a good judge of character.

I thought poorly of Atta, Pollux, and Jaysen when I met them, and look at us now. They mean more to me than my own family at this point.

Leon looks around at us. "This is a bit more people than you sent word of, Pollux." He gestures to us. "Which one is the girl?"

"This is Elliora," Pollux says, gesturing to me. His face, however, remains stoic. As if he doesn't want to show his feelings for me in front of Leon, or maybe I'm just imagining that.

"Hi, nice to meet you, Leon." I hold my hand out and shake his.

"Likewise," he says.

"We were just tying the horses together to make the crossing," Pollux states.

"Great, I'll help you." He starts walking towards the horses with Pollux.

Atta leans over and whispers, "I can't feel . . . anything from him."

"What?" I ask.

"I can't . . . there is no intuition, no intentions. He gives me . . . nothing." She moves her eyes from his retreating back to meet mine. "I've never had that before," she whispers.

"It's okay, maybe that's a good thing?" I'm trying to remain positive. It was my idea to flee the comfortable palace I was in and bring us all out here. Technically, it was Pollux's idea first, but I made the call.

I can only hope it was the right choice in the grand scheme of things. I still don't know the entire prophecy I'm meant to fulfill, and I'd like to learn more before being forced into a marriage with a shady Night King who says I'm supposed to bring about the 'Demise of Day.'

I reach down and give Atta's hand a squeeze. "You're the best . . . well, only friend I've ever had." I smile at her. "We will be fine if we stick together."

"Why, so I can protect your ass with my swords and daggers?" she laughs.

I laugh too: it's one of the reasons I love her, she's the only one who makes me laugh. "No, Atta, because we are stronger together. Also, I've been training for months, and so has Jaysen. We can wield swords; I just don't own one."

She looks at me for a minute, and then pulls one of the dual swords strapped to her back off, and begins strapping it on mine.

"Atta, what are you doing?" I ask.

"I'm giving you this sword. You should be able to protect yourself, Ellie. Every woman in this realm should own their own sword. This one is yours now." She gives me a sad smile.

"Atta . . . I . . ." I'm at a loss for words.

"Maybe if my parents had a sword, they would still be alive. Or maybe they wouldn't, but I couldn't live with myself if something happened to you. Especially if it was just because you didn't have a weapon on you." She finishes strapping the sword on my back.

"I have an extra thigh strap for daggers, too. I don't have extra daggers with me, but here, let's put the strap on now, and as soon as we can, we will get you your own set of daggers." She reaches up and squeezes my shoulders. "Now take good care of your new sword, it was once a very famous knight's sword."

"What? Why? How did you get it?" I ask. "And why in the gods would you give it to *me*?"

"How I got it is a story for another day," she winks, and walks away to help Pollux and Leon with the horses.

Jaysen must've gone to relieve himself or something during this time, because looking around, I don't see him anywhere.

I get one final stretch in, and then watch Atta, Pollux, and Leon prep. They are all discussing the mist, and I can only overhear a few words here and there.

Jaysen walks out from the trees to my left. I smile at him.

"You ready?" I ask him.

"Ready as I'll ever be." He smiles reluctantly, his usual happy-go-lucky demeanor missing.

Leon holds Pegasus by the reins in front of us. Pollux and I are seated on him. Pollux is complaining that my new addition of a sword is in his way.

I don't care, though, I'm so happy to have a weapon of my own. One that was given to me by my best friend.

Jaysen and Atta are behind us on Epona, who is currently tied to Pegasus for the journey.

No one is getting lost in there I repeat over and over in my head. I can't lose anyone. We are going to continue straight, and Leon is going to lead us through. We have a plan.

I breathe in through my nose and out through my mouth to prepare. I need to stay calm, for Pegasus, and for the group. If I am nervous and on edge, the others will quickly follow.

"Everyone ready?" Leon calls out.

"Yes," we all answer in unison.

And then we move.

Straight into the mist, where it is completely impossible to see. I blink a few times, trying to adjust my eyes to this new environment. The mist clings to the ground like a memory that refuses to fade. It curls low over the moss-covered stones and weaves over the gnarled roots of ancient trees. The air is thick with the scent of damp dirt and something older, something that whispers of buried secrets.

Each footstep the horses take is muffled, as though the fog itself is swallowing sound, leaving only the soft rhythm of our breath and the distant drip of unseen water. Shadows loom and shift with every step. Branches reach down like the arms of old spirits, beckoning us deeper into the mist.

The path, if it could still be called one, narrows beneath arching tree branches and vanishes into the gray. Occasional fragments of broken stone poke up from the ground, trying to cause chaos among us.

After about fifteen minutes of silent travel, a crumbling archway emerges. It's cloaked in ivy, and its stones are etched with symbols worn smooth by the wind and weather. We pause, and I hold my breath in anticipation. Leon's fingertips brush the ancient carvings. I can't tell what he's doing, and it's hard to see through the shadows and mist. Suddenly, I feel the pulse of something vast and watching.

The fog thickens around us.

A soft hum vibrates through the air, not the wind or a voice, but something that stirs beneath my skin. It's a sensation, a tingle at the base of my neck, a cold chill behind my eyes, and the pull of an invisible thread beckoning me forward.

Somewhere ahead, a faint, purple light begins to glow; it pulses in a steady and rhythmic beat, like a heartbeat. We continue on, deeper into the mist, each step creating more of a crossroads between what was and what might be for us.

And still, the mist whispers to me.

Chapter Twenty-Eight

I THINK I'M LOSING my mind. Or maybe I already have.

The moment Leon touched the symbols on the archway, something snapped. My head flooded with voices, too many to count. They are all whispering, shouting, and overlapping.

I'm doing my best to keep my expression neutral, to play it cool like nothing's wrong. But it's hard to fake calm when I can't even hear my own thoughts over all the noise.

The mist is thick. I'm hoping maybe they can't see my face through it. Either way, I hold it steady, just in case.

"How much further?" I groan, mumbling to Pollux.

"Are you okay?" he asks, as his hand that rests on my waist tightens.

"Yeah," I grunt. The pressure in my head feels like it will explode. I can barely hear anything he is saying.

The worst part is, the voices overlap so much I can't make out any of the words anyway. I've got 'ancient' and 'dark' a few times, but that is it.

I close my eyes, trusting that Pollux has me, and place my hands on Pegasus.

I try to focus on the movement of Pegasus, the steady rhythm. Anything but the noise.

I breathe in through my nose again, and out through my mouth.

I continue the pattern over and over.

I am the picture of calm on the exterior.

I suddenly feel the cool breeze shift. The wind halts, and the air feels stale.

I open my eyes: the mist is gone, the night sky no longer has stars, just dark gray clouds covering every surface. The air is chilled, but there is no breeze, not any more. The air feels weighted, and the ground is dark. As if the entire surface is covered in one giant shadow.

We keep moving forward, until Jaysen and Atta are out of the mists as well, and we all hop off the horses. I look around the dark new realm. I'm curious now why I couldn't witness the dark crossing a few months ago on the ship.

"Wow, that was rough," I mumble.

"What? Why?" Pollux asks. "Did I miss something?"

"What? You didn't hear the voices?" I ask.

He gives me an incredibly concerned look. I look at Atta and Jaysen who also both wear concerned expressions now.

"I . . . Uh . . ." I scratch the back of my neck, and stretch. "Okay, well should we continue to the . . . "

Atta jumps at me, pushing me to the ground. Pollux yells. Chaos erupts as Jaysen runs behind the horses to hide. I'm looking around, trying to figure out what is going on, when Atta falls to the ground next to me.

An arrow bulges out from between her ribs.

"Atta!" I scream.

I sit up and crawl across the muddy ground to her. "Atta!" I yell, picking up her upper body. Blood streams down her ribs.

"Help!" I yell. "Where in the gods is Leon? We need a healer. Help!" I can't stop yelling. Someone needs to help me.

Tears start streaming down my face. I can't lose Atta. Atta gave me everything. She gave me life. I didn't want to live before her friendship.

My eyes blur with all the tears.

"Someone, please!" I cry.

Pollux is in the distance fighting some soldiers that appeared out of nowhere. Jaysen crawls over.

"Oh gods," Jaysen mumbles. "I'm going to be sick." He gags at the sight of blood.

"Atta, you're okay. I'll find a healer, you'll be okay," I cry as I look down at her. She's losing a lot of blood now.

Her breathing is getting shallow, and I look at the arrow wedged in her. It probably punctured a lung, it's so deep. I try to pull it out for a second. Hoping I can get it out, and then hold pressure to stop the bleeding, but I can't. It's so deep.

I continue to sob. "Atta, please, stay with me okay?"

Atta looks at me and grabs my hand. She coughs, and blood comes out. "Ellie, it's my time."

"What? No! I'll find you a healer, Atta, please don't leave me." I sob more.

"Ellie, I knew I'd die coming here with you. I saw it in my future. I didn't know when, I was hoping I'd have time to teach you some new tricks, but I knew somehow, I would die for a good cause." She smiles up at me weakly. "Listen to me, you are meant to be in this realm. I can feel it in every fiber of my being. This is where you should be. Trust your gut, kid."

"Atta, I can't do this without you. Please, there has to be a way. We have to do something," I cry.

Pollux is still in the distance fighting. There looks to be about two soldiers left. It'll take him a minute, and then I'll have him get Atta on a horse and we can take her to a healer. There has to be one. I can save her, I know I can.

The dragon inside of me roars, begging to come out and burn those guards to the ground. I roar, in the form of a scream. It's painful, but I can't go on without her.

I continue to put pressure near the arrow, hoping I can get the bleeding to stop still.

Atta's breathing harder. "Ellie, look at me."

I look down at her in my lap. My hands covered in her blood, tears pouring from my eyes. I can barely see.

"You have to go on Ellie. You're the best friend I've had in years." Every word is broken up like she's struggling to get them out.

"Shh. Stop talking, I'll get you to a healer, you'll be fine," I cry.

Pollux finally comes over and kneels on the other side of Atta.

"Oh gods, Atta," he mumbles. He takes my hands and moves them, so he can continue to hold pressure.

"Pollux! Do something! We need to get her to a healer." I'm screaming irrationally, but I can't help it. We need to move. "Where is Leon?" I yell.

"I don't know, El. I can't find him," he says softly.

I'm annoyed by his softness. We need to move. We need to get Atta somewhere.

"Let's go, Pollux, pick her up, get her to a healer," I cry.

"El, I don't think there are healers in this realm . . ." he whispers.

"Pollux, there *has* to be. We *have* to save her. Let's go!" I cry, and yell. I don't understand why we aren't moving.

Atta's blood is everywhere. My hands are covered, the ground around me is covered. Her breathing is so shallow now, I can barely see her chest rise and fall.

My face hurts from all the tears.

Atta whispers, and every word sounds pained. "Ellie, you were my sunshine in a dark world. I knew you'd be special, but I didn't know just how special you would be, not only to the world, but to me. I've lived 227 years, it's my time, kid. I'll see you in the next world." Tears stream down her face.

I'm trying to process that she just said she is 227 years old, what does that even mean?

"Atta, please don't go. I need you," I cry.

Her breathing stops; her eyes are blank. There is no more life behind them.

I scream, I wail, I can't stop crying. I've never felt pain like this before.

I can't push the dragon down anymore. My fingertips begin to tremble, and the air around me thickens with an ancient power. My eyes, once bright and human, flicker, pupils narrowing into slits. A low hum fills the air, resonating from within my chest like a distant storm.

My breath catches, and my spine arches sharply as a cascade of shimmering scales ripple across my skin, consuming my soft flesh with an iridescent armor. Fingers stretch, crack, and curl into talons tipped with obsidian claws. Bones groan beneath my skin, reshaping, in a series of shuddering snaps. The sword, the one Atta gave me as a gift, pops off, and falls to the ground beside me.

Wings erupt from my back in a spray of light and shadow, unfurling with the grace of something ancient reborn. Membranes shimmer like stained glass caught in sunlight, pulsing with veins of silver and flame. My hair moves in the wind, and then vanishes as my head reshapes. My jawline extends, teeth sharpening into fangs capable of death.

I roar, and it's not the voice of a woman anymore. It's the sound of thunder rolling across a forgotten sky. It's the most pain I've ever felt in sound form. Smoke curls from my nostrils as horns crown my skull, majestic and terrible.

Where I once sat with Atta, trembling and scared, now towers my dragon form—vast, glorious, and unbound.

I'm no longer myself. I've removed myself and my pain from reality. I've pushed myself deep down, and fully given over to my dragon.

More guards from the Shadow Realm approach. I stretch my wings out like dark thunderclouds, and claw the mud beneath my feet. I rear back my head, and a low, guttural growl rumbles from my chest, building into a deep, thunderous roar.

I am so angry. Atta was the family member I was never lucky enough to have. All I can feel is rage pulsing under my scales. Pollux shouts, but whatever he says, I don't listen. I can't hear him, I'm too far gone. And honestly, I don't care what he has to say. My anger consumes me.

With a sudden, violent exhale, I unleash a torrent of fire. Flames erupt from my open jaws. They are brilliant orange and searing white at the core. They light up the entire sky like a sudden sunrise. The blaze roars forward in a wide arc, turning the moist air around us into a shimmering heat. It scorches everything in its path. The trees are instantly engulfed, the stones blacken, and the ground cracks beneath the blast.

The fire seems almost alive, coiling and writhing like a living thing as it pours from my throat. Smoke billows around me, cloaking me in a haze of heat and shadow. In that moment, I feel a sense of awe and terror at what I've become. I've unleashed a pure, primal power.

Suddenly, I feel something stab my core. I look down. In my dragon form, it looks too small, I can't reach it. My vision starts to blacken at the edges, and I sway.

The last thing I remember is Pollux screaming "El!"

Chapter Twenty-Nine

I WAKE IN THE back of a carriage. I look down at my body: human. I sigh and glance around. Pollux is passed out to my right, and Jaysen is out cold to my left.

There are no holes, or windows in the carriage. There is also no Atta. My chest aches.It feels impossible to breathe. I never would've left the palace if I knew Atta would die.

I wonder when Atta knew. She said she knew she would die. I wonder if she knew before or after we left the palace.

I feel angry and sad at the same time. It feels like being caught in a storm where the wind pulls me in opposite directions. It's a tight knot in my chest, the grief weighing me down, while my rage bubbles just beneath the surface. I feel hollow, like the most important thing has been taken from me, and yet my blood boils because it shouldn't have happened in the first place.

It feels like I want to scream and cry at the same time. The sadness makes me feel vulnerable, hurt, and even helpless. But my anger gives me an edge, a rage that wants to lash out, and find a reason this all happened. Or at the very least, find someone to blame.

The war of my emotions is exhausting. I'm being pulled between needing comfort and wanting justice. I'm not even sure which feeling is stronger, or which one makes more sense. But they're both there coiled up inside me, fighting for space.

I wonder if I should end it all and go join Atta in the next world. It has to be better than this one, it has to be easier.

I look at Pollux and Jaysen then, and realize I can't end it. At least, not yet. I have a few more members of my chosen family to keep safe. I couldn't keep Atta safe, but I'm going to try and keep these two safe.

The carriage jolts over a hill, or boulder. I fly up a little, and land down on my back. I groan, as the jolt accentuates my body's aches. I forgot what a toll my dragon shift takes on my body.

Although, I don't feel nearly as beat down as the first time I shifted, so some part of my training must be working.

The jolt wakes Pollux and Jaysen, both groaning and rubbing at their temples.

Jaysen slowly sits up. "Oh gods, Elliora. Are you okay?"

I look down at my charred, muddy, blood-covered body. "I'm . . . not, but we will get through this together."

I can't even force a smile like I usually can.

"Where are we?" Jaysen asks.

I shrug. "In some kind of carriage. No windows or openings, so not sure where we are heading."

Jaysen groans. "I just want to go home. I want to see my parents, my little sister, and my older brother. I want to see the sun." Jaysen starts crying abruptly.

It's odd, I've never seen him anything but happy or scared. I reach over and give his hand a gentle squeeze. "I know, we will get you back there someday . . ."

Pollux finally sits up, groaning, and grabbing at his chest.

"Are you okay?" I ask.

"Fine," Pollux snaps.

I'm not sure what to say. He seems angry, but at what? Maybe it's the same reason I'm angry. I want revenge. I want to know who killed the best friend I've ever had, the only friend I've ever loved. I want to kill everyone they love, and then them. I want to burn them all to the ground.

"We are heading for the Citadel," Pollux grumbles.

"Citadel?" I question. I've never heard the terminology before.

"Ah, yes, similar to a palace, but it's more of a fortress, and protects most of the residents of the Shadow Realm," he explains.

"Hm, okay. How do you know that's where we are heading?" I ask.

"It's the only place they would take us. To see the King of the Shadow Realm," he states.

"Weren't you taking us there anyway?" I ask.

"Yeah . . ." he whispers.

"What aren't you telling me?" I accuse.

"El . . . I . . ." he stutters.

He's interrupted by loud banging, and the carriage halts. I sit up and wait impatiently for the back carriage door to open.

"I think I'm going to be sick," Jaysen groans.

"Not now, you fool," Pollux seethes.

"Pollux! Calm down, he can't control that. He's nervous and we just witnessed . . ." I trail off, I can't even speak of it. It still doesn't feel real. It feels like she will be back here any second.

My stomach bottoms out and threatens to revolt as well. I practice my breathing again, in through my nose, and out through my mouth.

I can do this. Atta told me too, she said I was *meant* to be here.

Suddenly, the back door opens, and Leon stands there looking smug.

"Why you . . ." I stand and aggressively make my way towards him. As soon as I reach the end of the carriage, though, a dark magic holds me firmly in place.

Shadows wrap around my wrists like handcuffs, holding me in there. "What in the gods is this?" I shout.

"Welcome to the Shadow Realm, Elliora," he smirks.

"You are a piece of shit." I spit at him, but even the spit gets stopped by a moving shadow, protecting his face from my saliva.

I roar, or rather, the dragon within me does.

I'm so absolutely angry at this man.

I no longer give a fuck what Jaysen knows, and I shift.

My breathing slows, my spine arches as though pulled by some invisible thread. My skin begins to glisten, no longer smooth, but scaled.

My fingers curl unnaturally, melting into one another, and my bones soften and restructure, until my arms are no longer arms but coils—sleek, muscular, and fluid.

My forked tongue flickers, tasting the air with a predatory awareness. My legs vanish beneath me, consumed by a tail that coils.

I am gone. In my place, a great serpent writhes in silence, its sleek form pulsing with power, coiled and ready to attack. I slither under the shadows, and Leon yelps.

I hope he is scared. I hope he feels so much pain.

I slither down and coil under the carriage, watching through my narrowed eyes, tracking Leon's every movement.

It's hard when I'm this low to the ground, the shadows here are thicker, and harder to see through.

Leon shouts, "Gods, I knew this girl would be a huge problem."

He starts moving toward the carriage. I hear him shut the door above me, trapping Jaysen and Pollux in again. I slither out from under, and as quickly as I possibly can, I find his leg, curl around it, and bite.

Leon screams, and falls to the ground. I uncoil myself from him and move back under the carriage.

I let my body slowly shift back into my human form, but as soon as I do, shadows curl around my ankles and wrists holding me tightly in place.

Even though I'm a prisoner, I smile.

I've come really far since that first day I shifted.

Leon yells at all the guards, "Get her to the palace, get them to the king, *now*. I'm completely sick of them. I don't want anything to do with that dreadful wannabe goddess again," he hisses.

My stomach flips, the king. The king is likely responsible for ordering them to kill Atta. It's his fault. I'm sure it is. One guard opens the carriage door, and another throws me back in with Pollux and Jaysen.

They slam the door shut again.

Pollux starts yelling, "El, what in all the realms were you thinking? Why would you do that?"

I turn and glare at him. "Because Atta is dead. Atta is dead because of Leon, and I'd be happy to kill him for that. In fact, I hope my snake form is venomous. I hope he dies from my bite."

Pollux looks at me with concern. "El, this isn't you."

"It is now," I say.

Chapter Thirty

The carriage is quiet when it starts moving again.

Jaysen still looks sick, like he could pass out again at any second. He leans his head against the side of the carriage, eyes on the ground, breathing heavily.

Pollux still glares at me, like I've become an evil monster.

Maybe I have. All I know is, I want revenge. I need something—anything—to make this right. Atta meant more to me than anyone or anything ever has. And someone's going to pay for taking that away from me.

Tears begin streaming down my face before I can stop them. I focus on my breathing, and push all the feelings down.

I can't feel these things right now. I need to focus on the road ahead.

I look back at Pollux. "Any idea what lies ahead?"

He still looks angry with me, but mumbles, "Yes and no."

"Want to fill us in, or should we just be surprised?" I snap.

"You need to calm down before we head into the king, El. He's going to be upset, and he is incredibly powerful," he whispers.

"I need to calm down?" I seethe.

"Yes, El. I know you're upset, I know you're grieving, and you have every right to be. We will make a plan later. But, you need to go into this meeting levelheaded," he says.

I roll my eyes, and lie down against the floor of the carriage. I close my eyes, and think about the stars. For some odd reason, it still brings me peace. I know the Night Realm had its issues, but I will really miss the stars. The sense of calm and understanding they brought me.

I don't know who Pollux is right now. He's clearly hiding something, and I wish Atta was here to tell me whether I can trust him or not.

Isn't that sad? Pollux is my lover at this point, and for some reason, I still don't fully trust him. I still get the sense he is keeping vital information from me.

Jaysen groans. I open my eyes and peek over at him. He looks like shit, so I hand him a random canteen of water. "Drink some water, Jaysen."

His hand shakes as he brings the canteen to his lips, but he manages to get some down.

I'm worried about Jaysen, too, even though I don't trust him fully either. I can't lose either of these guys right now.

The emotional pain within me tells me to let go and trust them both. We have to trust each other to move on.

Pollux reaches over and squeezes my hand. "I've messed up a lot today. I'm grieving, too. I've known Atta a long time . . . she was my friend, even before you came into our lives. I'm not handling this well either, but we need to stay strong for what is coming."

"How long did you know her? She said she was . . . 227 years old?" I whisper.

"I've known her for almost one hundred years," Pollux whispers.

My eyes feel like they might bulge out from their sockets. "Who in the gods are you? You said you're from the Shadow Realm . . ."

"I am," Pollux states.

"Then why were you in the Night Realm for one hundred years? And how old are you?" I question.

"Surprisingly, I'm younger than Atta, I'm 150. I was sent to the Night Realm to wait for you, the one from the prophecy," he says.

My mind is reeling, I'm exhausted, and I don't understand why everyone has been waiting for me all this time.

"How do you know I'm the one from the prophecy?" I ask quietly.

He smiles. "Well, you're beautiful, part-day and part-night. You can shift into anything, correct? The stars worship you, they glow within you. They are part of you."

"And that was all in this prophecy?" I ask.

"Well, most of it," he mumbles.

"So, why should I be in the Shadow Realm? Why shouldn't I have stayed in the Night Realm and married the king? Wasn't that the prophecy?" I ask.

"No, that's the king's twisted version of the prophecy," Pollux seethes.

"And who's to say the Shadow King hasn't twisted his own? What if you're leading me to another twisted king?" I question. "What if every realm has formed its own version of this so-called prophecy? Where does the original prophecy exist?"

"I'm not . . . I don't know actually . . ." he says quietly.

"Well, I'm going to find out," I state. "So, why lead me here? What makes the Shadow Realm better than the Night Realm? What makes this king better than the last?"

"I don't. . . although . . . I don't know, I'm starting to wish I hadn't led you here at all," he whispers.

"What, why?" I shriek.

The carriage halts again.

There is so much noise from the outside.

A guard swings open the back door.

"We're here," the largest man says, " and the king will see you now."

We all stand. I have to help Jaysen up, and he leans into me a little as we walk.

The second we pass the exit of the carriage, dark shadows bind our wrists. They also bind us all together by the waist.

We turn north when I see it.

My eyes widen at the sight, as Pollux whispers, "Welcome home, El."

The giant Citadel before me looks like nothing I've ever seen. It looms like a jagged wound against a bruised sky, its towers piercing the mist like blackened spears. Perched atop a steep cliff, the fortress seems to grow from the rock itself—its obsidian walls slick with moisture and veiled in creeping ivy that moves as though it's alive. Narrow windows glow faintly with a cold, unnatural light, suggesting life within.

The massive iron gates before me are black and spiked, and hang crooked on ancient hinges. On both sides of the gates are crumbling statues of long-forgotten kings, their stone faces eroded into grotesque masks. The air around the Citadel hums with a silent tension, heavy with the weight of old magic and the echo of a thousand whispered secrets. Crows circle overhead, silent and watchful, as if waiting for something to stir beneath the stone.

I've seen enough now to know, those crows could very well be shifting guards. Nothing would surprise me anymore.

A guard shoves us forward, and speaks in a menacing tone. "Time to go meet your new king."

Chapter Thirty-One

WE ENTER THE UMBRA Citadel, and my hands are clammy. My pulse races, and it feels like there is a knot tightening in my stomach. My steps are hesitant and unsure. My mind races with one question—*Am I ready?*.

I notice my heartbeat speeding up, and my breath becoming shallow. Every detail of this unfamiliar space weighs on my mind as I take in the scene around me, the lighting, the layout, and the unfamiliar faces. It feels as if I'm hyper-aware of everything, and yet unable to focus on anything clearly.

Still, despite the tension, there's a flicker of hope beneath my nerves, an inner push to keep moving forward, one step at a time. I glance at Pollux next to me, who looks the picture of calm. I look over to Jaysen on my other side, who still looks like complete shit, and isn't nearly as calm as Pollux. I honestly think he is just grateful to be here and be alive after everything that has happened.

I, on the other hand, am feeling almost every emotion. I am raging inside about Atta. My dragon form begs to come out and burn this place to the fucking ground. I'm feeling nervous about the thought of possible torture for my friends and myself. I'm feeling full of grief and sadness, and down toward the very bottom of my soul is a bit of excitement. Atta told me I was meant to be here. Pollux welcomed me home. I'm anxious to understand what that all means.

My stomach drops, and I almost throw up. I tell myself to think about Atta later, I *will* get my revenge on her behalf, but now is not the time to grieve. I need to be the best version of myself before we meet this King of Shadows.

I have no idea what to expect. He is obviously a savage ruler who demands his guards instantly kill one of us upon entry just to 'prove a point.' Which is what I'm assuming happened since I haven't heard a valid explanation yet.

Other than the few offhanded comments from Pollux about the king, I really don't know what to expect. I wish I knew more. I wish I had some idea of who, or what, I am about to face.

I also wish I wasn't covered in mud, sweat, tears, and blood. I wish I didn't have half of my clothes charred off from my angry flames.

There is no changing anything now.

The doors swing open into a vast, awe-inspiring chamber. Towering walls are cloaked in dark, dramatic murals. There are night skies swirling with stars, fierce dragons mid-flight, epic battles frozen in time, and watchful owls perched in shadowed corners. The ceiling soars overhead, a canopy of glass framed by crisscrossing black beams, casting shifting patterns of light and shadow across the floor.

At the far end of the room, a young man sits upon a towering throne. It's an impossible structure, crafted to resemble a living shadow. The black throne coils and curves at its base, stretching like smoke around the raised dais, as if it grew from the darkness itself.

As we get closer, I stop suddenly. It can't be possible.

I glance at Pollux next to me. As his eyes meet mine, they are full of sorrow.

I look back at the man on the throne.

I'm . . . lost. I'm stunned. I can't make my brain form words.

The man on the throne . . . is Pollux. He is identical to Pollux, the only difference being the color of his eyes, the length of his hair, and the color of his hair.

Every other feature is identical.

I look back to Pollux, who bows his head full of remorse, as he whispers, "I wanted to tell you El, I . . . "

"Silence!" the man on the throne bellows.

The room practically vibrates with the sound.

I swallow.

I haven't been super nervous much since the first day I shifted to a dragon. Most things seem so small in comparison now. I've felt invincible, like I had nothing to lose.

Right now, though, I'm nervous.

You can *feel* power emanating all around the room.

There is a dark hum in the air, that tickles my skin, and makes my hair stand on end.

I look back to the man on the throne, as he smiles. It should send a chill down my spine, but instead, butterflies take flight in my stomach.

"Hello Elliora, brother, and . . . you." He glances to Jaysen, who looks like he is about to pass out at any second.

His eye contact returns to me, and I feel a buzz of electricity skate along my spine. It's hard not to think he is the most gorgeous man I've ever seen.

He is identical to Pollux, but with beautiful blue-gray eyes and short dark black hair. His muscles are almost more toned than Pollux's, even though before this moment, I would've considered that a nearly impossible feat.

He wears a sleeveless shirt, showing off said muscles, and his arms are covered in black ink. The swirling dark lines run along almost every curve of muscle. It's hard not to want to trace them. I bring my gaze back up to his eyes, and he smirks.

"I've waited so long for this," he says, his voice a caress, floating gently over my skin.

I'm temporarily in a haze, before I snap out of it, and my eyes snap to Pollux, who has dropped to his knees beside me. His head is bowed down toward the floor, hands on his one knee as he kneels before this king.

"Forgive me, brother, for it took much longer than I anticipated for her to arrive in the Night Realm. It also took longer than predicted to get her out of the Night Realm, and into your Kingdom," he states loudly.

"What in all the gods are you talking about?" I seethe.

Pollux looks over at me, golden eyes full of sorrow and guilt. "I'm so sorry El, but this was the plan all along."

My stomach bottoms out. My fists curl and shake. I'm actively preventing myself from shifting due to my rage. My wolf growls at the surface, and I quickly realize, they are trapped. I can't shift in this damned Citadel.

I swing my gaze back to the man on the throne. The rage simmering under my skin threatens to make my knees buckle. This king seems to notice that my body is struggling under the pressure. That I've just realized I can't shift here. He smirks at me.

His gaze moves back to Pollux next to me, just as Pollux looks up at his brother. "She is exactly what we expected, Castor, but more beautiful than we ever imagined."

Castor claps his hands together slowly. "Great performance, brother! Wonderful, stunning, and I would expect nothing less from you. But when will you tell me how you fucked her?"

Jaysen tumbles to the floor next to me, out cold. I reach over to help him up, but Castor yells, "Leave him! Do not touch that . . . boy."

I stand up straight, and glare at Castor.

He glares back.

His eyes move back to Pollux. "I'm waiting."

He twirls his finger around the end of his dark throne, with a bored look on his face.

Pollux stares mouth agape in shock. "I . . . well . . ."

"You didn't think I'd find out?" he says with menace. "You didn't think I'd *know*? I know everything. You know that. How. Dare. You."

"Please, brother, let me explain," Pollux begs.

I realize quickly that Pollux wasn't just not telling me the whole truth; he actively led me into a trap.

Castor snaps and gets the attention of one of the many guards near him. A man runs over to his side. "Wasat, please take my brother to the dungeons and poison him. Leave him to die there."

My stomach revolts. I'm going to be sick. Is this man really going to kill his own brother?

"Yes, sir," the guard responds.

"NO!" I scream. I fall to my knees next to Pollux. Turning to grab his face, I yell, "Why did you bring me here to this monster? How could you hide the fact that this king is your *brother*? That this was your plan? I deserve a fucking answer."

Pollux locks eyes with me, and tries to put a hand on my cheek. He's stopped by the shadows around his wrist. "I told you before, El, I shouldn't have ever wanted this. I said it that night in the tent. This thing with you, it was forbidden in every way, yet, I couldn't stop myself. I tried, I really did try to keep things between us professional. It was all completely worth it, though. The world around us is completely falling apart, and yet, I don't care. You are everything I need." He sighs. "I knew by loving you, our time together would end. I knew it, and I did it anyway. But El, I promise, you will be loved and cared for again, and you *are* worthy of it. My time in this world is done, but I'll love you again in the next one."

It's the first time he has said the word *love*, and I guess I felt it too, although I didn't know what love was. I don't think I ever have. A tear runs down my cheek.

I turn to Castor. "Don't do this! He is your brother!" The tears start flowing now. One after the other, they stream down my face.

I'm not just angry, I'm full of rage. I've lost Atta, and now this man says he loves me and he's going to die. I finally found my family.

"Please," I plead.

Castor locks eyes with me, and his expression softens. For a minute I think he's going to change his mind. For one single moment, I think I'm going to get a happy ending.

His face shifts though, and the rage returns.

"Wasat, kill him here, now," Castor seethes.

Wasat lifts his sword and drives it right into Pollux's heart.

"No!" The scream that tears from my throat causes the ground to shake. I grab onto Pollux, and hold him, tears pouring out of my eyes at such a rapid pace, I can't even see his last breath.

"I love you too," I whisper as I press my forehead against his.

I hold him, rocking back and forth as I cry.

Minutes and minutes of total agony pass. My body threatens to shift over and over, but I can't. I want to burn the stupid Shadow King to the ground. My body threatens to pass out, but I hold it together, remembering Pollux's words from the carriage. He was so damned worried about me holding it together.

I can't believe this man waited until his dying breath to tell me he loved me. Emotions roll through my body in waves.

I turn and look at this *king,* who is still sitting comfortably on the throne.

"How dare you." I lock eyes with Castor. I lift my hand and point at him. "You will pay for this, for all of it. For Atta. For Pollux. I will come after everyone you love, and I will kill them all. I will make you watch, I will make you pay. And after all the torture, I promise I will kill you," I seethe.

The asshole smiles.

"I hate you." I spit. It's a promise, and he finally flinches. It's the only thing that he has reacted to since we walked into this godforsaken room. He looks like *that* is the one thing that actually pained him to hear.

So I keep going.

"Why?" I scream. "Why in all the gods' names would you kill your own brother?" I demand. "I deserve an answer!"

"He was scum. He did not do as his realm asked. He did not follow the directions I gave him nearly a century ago. He played both sides for his own personal gain. But most importantly, he touched what is *mine.* He loved what is mine, and he *knew.* He knew the whole damn time," he fumes. "He loved my *mate.*"

Epilogue

King Canis

I ALWAYS KNEW POLLUX was playing both sides.

He thought he was so slick and smart. He thought he had me fooled. I let him think it all these years, let him think I'm a silly weak king who can only shift into a dragon.

While he thought he was tricking me and playing both sides, I was truly the one tricking him. I know all about his plans, about his quest to find what is rightfully mine, and steal it.

He thinks I'm a fool, but he has walked right into my trap.

I sit across the table from Arcturus, some silly child from the Day Realm. I cannot fathom why the world continues to torture me in this way. Why would the gods punish me by sending two ignorant kids to fulfill a century-old prophecy?

I sigh, as this stupid child continues to ask obsolete questions, like . . . *why do I have to?* Who does he think he is? I'm a king, for gods' sake, he will do as I say, for eternity. The quicker he learns that, the easier this is.

Tate swings the door open aggressively, and I stand. Arcturus stands up too, and turns toward the door.

Tate smiles, and then bows.

"I take it they have fled the palace?" I ask quietly.

"Yes, Your Grace. They are on their way to the stables now," he says with a smirk.

"Excellent," I grin, and resume sitting.

Arcturus stares at me, confused, but sits back down because I point, gesturing he should do so.

"Uh, Your Grace?" Tate says, with an air of concern.

"Yes?" I ask.

"There is one small hiccup. They have left the palace with two others, Ataksak and some kid from the Day Realm named Jaysen," he states.

I raise an eyebrow. Atta, I assumed. I know enough about all of them to have seen that one coming. This Jaysen kid, well, that one confuses me still, but he is nothing but a thorn in my side. He poses no threat, and holds no magic. So I remain unconcerned and unbothered by this news.

"Thank you for the updates, Sir Tate. No one has seen or made contact with the prisoner still, correct?" I question.

"That is correct, Your Grace," he answers.

"Wonderful, thank you, you serve your realm well." I smile at him, and nod my head.

Tate turns to leave the room. "Oh Taterfall, one more thing, please make sure no one heads after them. We know where they are going. If someone reports it, tell them not to pursue." I gesture that he can leave now.

He bows one final time, while saying, "Yes, Your Grace."

He closes the door behind him.

Arcturus still looks concerned, and I sigh. "What, Arcturus? Your confusion is bothering me. What troubles your mind?"

Arcturus twists his hands together, a nervous tick he shares with another. Both of which drive me mad.

He finally speaks, "Your Grace, it's just, I don't understand. If she is the one from the prophecy, the one you need, why am I here? And why are you letting her go? Why aren't we going after her?"

I grin. "Oh, sweet Arcturus, you have so much to learn. When I gave you all that speech in the training Colosseum, did you hear nothing? Let me remind you, I stated we were looking for the one who would fulfill the prophecy, the one who had dark magic coursing through their veins." I gesture to him.

His veins are now black, and coursing with the dark magic we need.

I smile. "And then I said we were *also* looking for the one in the prophecy to be my wife. The one to help me save the realms and be my wife, that's not you . . . that's her." I gesture in the direction of the stables, knowing she is likely there by now.

"Then why let her go?" he questions.

I don't like being questioned by some half-a-brain farmer from the Day Realm. It annoys me, so I snap at him, "You have a lot to learn here, Arcturus, do not strike a tone with me."

He bows his head toward the floor. "I'm sorry, Your Grace, I'm just struggling to understand why you let the one who is supposed to be your wife flee the castle with another man . . . "

"I let her go, to become the *real* one from the prophecy. I need her to be rageful, spiteful, and evil at her very core," I say, smiling, "and Pollux will do that to her, Pollux will bring her such absolute rage, such undeniable grief, that she will have no choice but to become the killer she was always destined to be."

I think for a moment, wondering if I should share any more, whether this nitwit in front of me deserves any more information than what I've already given.

It hits me, the last piece of the puzzle, the last move in the game of chess I've been playing all these years.

"Arcturus, you are one half of a whole." I pick up the two moon pieces in front of me, "You are one half of a prophecy, *and* you are the half-brother of Elliora Polaris. You both share the same father, who resides right here, in the Night Realm."

*Elliora's story will continue... *cue Taylor Swift's The Prophecy**

@gloinkdesigns

While the dedication is for everyone, this book is *actually* for my bestest buddy, Barney. Barney was the absolute best dog family dog the past twelve and a half years, and passed shortly after I finished editing this book. This one is for you sweet boy, we miss your endless snuggles. We are happy you get to play with my baby Sophie again. You were truly LEGEND...wait for it...DAIRY.

Acknowledgements

I REALLY NEVER THOUGHT I'd write and publish a book.

Yet, here I am doing it twice in one year.

First and foremost, I would like to thank my husband. Not only are you my best friend in the whole world, and the best decision I've ever made— you're my number one fan now. The fact that you not only read my first book in three days, but continue to reference it and love it means the world. You make love and marriage easy, and I couldn't do a single thing in this world without you. Thank you for peer pressuring me to finally write my fantasy book. Without your support, I truly wouldn't have done it.

To my kiddos, my little Peanut and Pickle—please always know your mom loves you more than all the stars in the sky. I'm so proud of you both, and the people you are becoming. You can both do absolutely *anything* you put your mind to! Your excitement to hold my book in your hands and tell everyone your mom is an author has meant the absolute world. I know you will both do amazing things in this life!!

For the readers, thank you. Truly, from the bottom of my heart. You'll never know my gratitude for you taking the time to read this book, or any other book I write. It means the absolute world to me.

To my parents, thank you for encouraging me, for ordering my first book, and supporting me every step of the way. Thank you for always telling me I could be anything I wanted. I love you both.

Jenessa, my author bestie, neighbor, and life twin—I really couldn't have done this one without you. I think I would've stuck to rom-coms and never wrote the fantasy book in my head without our nighttime walks. I know I say it a lot, but I mean it when I say I want to be you when I grow up. You are incredible in *every* way. I cannot wait until you make it big and we get to celebrate your massive success!

Cassidy, thank you for ALPHA reading the hell out of this book. I know you didn't have the time or energy—but you did it anyway. I'll forever be grateful. Your edits and commentary made me keep going when I second-guessed all my life choices. I don't think I would've finished making this book without you.

Books & Banter, aka the Book Besties, I still don't know how I got so lucky. It still blows my mind and makes me laugh to think about it. Our little cult full of book-loving women is everything to me. I don't know where I'd be without you guys, but I know it wouldn't be half as fun. I love all of you, and your endless support.

Shout-out to all the independent and locally owned coffee shops I frequented during the writing of this book—you're superior in every way. But extra special shoutouts to The Bookish Shop in Gilbert, The Kind

Bean in Chandler, and Beanchain Coffee in Mesa for your amazing support after the release of my first book.

Thank you to my sweet author friend, Emily Shacklette, whose spicy books should be in every romance-lover's home library. Your support and virtual friendship is something I am so thankful for!

Thank you to Athira, at @gloinkdesigns, for working on ALL the art for this book. You made every character exactly the way I imagined them. I cannot thank you enough for your countless hours making these characters come to life.

Thank you to Sam Stringert, for being the best editor. Dealing with e-mails of my spiraling, and telling me to write the damn book anyways. Wouldn't be able to successfully publish this book without you!

Thank you Amanda @ Eternal Geekery, for putting so much love and care into making the beautiful fantasy map of this world!

Thank you to Megan, @lemonlee.shop for always putting up with my "HEY HERE ME OUT" texts. You are a magical human who deserves every good thing that comes your way. No Notes. It will now forever be a classic Megan and Ashley mess around.

Thank you to Chelsey and Cass for BETA reading, and screaming at me. You are amazing friends and I'm so incredibly grateful for you both.

Special shoutout to Tater the cat, who I unintentionally named a character after, but definitely deserves to have a character named after him. Long live Sir Tot.

about the AUTHOR

Ashley Claire is a cliché millennial Disney adult and hardcore Swiftie. Residing in hell.. Oops, I mean sunny Arizona, she is the mother of two amazing kids and married to her best friend. She has always been an avid reader with a passion for books. Ashley started her journey teaching high school and eventually moved on to be an editor and content writer for many years before deciding to drop everything and risk it all by writing her own stories and novels.

Ashley enjoys coffee, nerds gummy clusters, and pickles. She loves planning and hosting book clubs, and hopes everyone finds a group of bookish friends to share life with. The more book clubs in the world–- the merrier!

Follow along for updates on what Ashley has planned next!
Instagram: @ashleyclairebooks
Facebook: ashleyclairebooks
Website: www.ashleyclairebooks.com

www.ingramcontent.com/pod-product-compliance
Lightning Source LLC
Chambersburg PA
CBHW050029120726
47903CB00006B/1972